AND THE
SKELETON KING

Also by JeromeASF:

Bacca and the Riddle of the Diamond Dragon

AN UNOFFICIAL NOVEL

BACCA
AND THE
SKELETON KING

AN UNOFFICIAL MINECRAFTER'S ADVENTURE

JeromeASF

WITH SCOTT KENEMORE

SKY PONY PRESS
NEW YORK

Sky Pony Press books may be purchased in bulk at special discounts
for sales promotion, corporate gifts, fund-raising, or educational
purposes. Special editions can also be created to specifications.
For details, contact the Special Sales Department, Sky Pony Press,
307 West 36th Street, 11th Floor, New York, NY 10018 or
info@skyhorsepublishing.com.

Sky Pony® is a registered trademark of Skyhorse Publishing, Inc.®, a
Delaware corporation.

Minecraft® is a registered trademark of Notch Development AB.

The Minecraft game is copyright © Mojang AB.

Visit our website at www.skyponypress.com.

10 9 8 7 6 5 4 3 2 1

Manufactured in Canada, December 2015

Library of Congress Cataloging-in-Publication Data is available on file.

Cover design by Brian Peterson
Cover artwork by Josh Bruce (www.inkbyte.net)

Print ISBN: 978-1-5107-0902-7
Ebook ISBN: 978-1-5107-0903-4

Printed in Canada

CHAPTER ONE

All was quiet in the valley.

The warm breeze blew softly across the shimmering green landscape of the Overworld. The clouds hung low in the sky. Night had just fallen. The surrounding hills were covered in a thick green lawn. The breeze gently rustled each blade of grass.

. . . which completely hid the footsteps of the approaching horde.

At the edge of the valley, a peaceful crafter named Brian walked out the back door of his house and carefully closed it behind him. He had crafted his modest home out of red sandstone blocks from a nearby mesa. Brian made a living as an expert smelter, specializing in making iron ingots. Each day, he turned hundreds of blocks of iron ore into ingots which he sold to other crafters. Throughout the Overworld, there were few iron ingots finer than his.

After a long day of smelting, Brian liked to eat his dinner outside in the moonlight. There was a pleasant view of the valley from the back of his house, and Brian enjoyed it very much. However, this night was not to be like other ones. As Brian's nose took in the fragrant evening air, he noticed that something seemed a little bit off. Staring down into the beautiful green valley usually gave him a deep sense of calm. Yet tonight, he found that he could not relax. Danger was on the wind. Danger, and the scent of . . . Was that *bones*?

"Do bones have a smell?" Brian wondered out loud. He couldn't recall the last time he had smelled one on purpose. Whenever he cooked himself a rabbit stew, he usually just threw the bones straight into the trash.

But no. Something told him that the strange odor on the wind tonight was *definitely* bones.

"That's very strange," Brian said.

Then it got stranger.

The wind shifted directions, and Brian began to detect a *second* smell. It seemed to be coming from the opposite side of the valley. It was much stronger. And it was much, *much* worse.

This second smell carried the distinctive stench of rotting flesh. Of decay. Of gross, way-past-the-expiration-date meat, and other nasty things that were very unpleasant to think about.

Brian wrinkled his nose. Usually, his valley smelled wonderful at dusk, but tonight, something had completely ruined all of that. Yet what concerned Brian most of all was that these smells— both of them—seemed to be getting stronger by the minute. Which meant that something was getting *closer*.

Then Brian heard the moans.

From one side of the valley, a chorus of deep, low moans began to accompany the awful smells. Brian was an experienced crafter who had lived in many different parts of the Overworld, and he understood right away that this sound could mean only one thing. *Zombies.*

Brian knew these pests very well. They came out at night and sometimes wandered into your neighborhood. They could be a real nuisance—disturbing the landscaping, knocking things over, and generally being annoying. On top of everything else, they liked to attack unsuspecting people they came across, especially crafters. On the upside, they were slow, and usually easy to avoid. Brian could always retreat inside his sandstone house whenever he spotted one headed his way.

But Brian had a sneaking suspicion that whatever was making its way toward him was no normal mob of zombies.

Moments later, this sneaking suspicion was proved right.

As the smelter looked on, the largest group of zombies he had ever seen crested the hill on the east side of his valley. It was more than a mob—more than several mobs. It was a small army.

Rows and rows of hungry-looking zombies lined up at the lip of the valley. Several of them carried weapons, and many wore armor. Two or three even rode chickens. They all had mean, angry-looking expressions on their faces.

Brian was almost too astounded to feel afraid. What on earth were all of these zombies doing here? How had they all come together like this? What could they possibly want? Why were the chickens okay with this??

Then the answer (well, not to *every* question) loped into view.

From the corner of his eye, Brian suddenly detected movement on the *opposite* side of the valley. He turned and saw something even more astounding. Another army! This one was entirely made up of skeletons. Rows and rows of the bony things were carefully lining themselves up facing the zombies. Their bones gleamed brightly in the moonlight, and their bows made loud 'clack'-sounds as they jostled against one another.

Having no eyebrows or lips—or, really, faces at all—it was usually hard for Brian to get an idea of a skeleton's facial expression. But on this night, things were different. Each one of the skeletons' bony skulls found a way to look really, really angry!

Brian swallowed hard.

Like most crafters, Brian didn't particularly like zombies *or* skeletons. He might have said some bad things about them to other crafters. Okay, he *definitely* had. And sure, now and then he liked to try out a new weapon by bashing some skeletons or smacking some zombies with it. In fact, just last week he'd received a new golden sword as a birthday present from his brother. The first thing he'd done was to go looking for some zombies to try it out on. A fact he now deeply regretted.

But on the other hand, it wasn't like Brian was some kind of special *undead-hunter*. Plenty of crafters had spent more time than him shooting at zombies with arrows or whacking away at skeletons with a nice sharp axe. Why both mobs would choose to get together and gang up on him was completely beyond Brian.

Brian nervously rubbed his hands together and wondered what to do. Were they coming for him? Should he run back inside his house, shut the door, and hope all the monsters just went away? Should he flee from the valley entirely, even though it was his home? Should he break his golden sword over his knee and tell the zombies he was really, really sorry and he'd never do it again?

As Brian tried to figure out how we could possibly make it through the night alive, the zombie army and the skeleton army did something very strange. It was something that Brian had never known zombies or skeletons to do in the history of Minecraft. Ever. It was something unexpected. Something unprecedented.

And something—Brian reckoned as he looked on in mounting confusion—that might just change the Overworld forever.

CHAPTER TWO

Bacca stood at the center of the improvised crafting workshop in the garden that framed the front of his estate.

Bacca's enormous castle loomed in the background. Its high turrets cast a welcome shadow that kept everyone shaded from the hot sun. It was a gorgeous summer day. The breeze softly tousled Bacca's fur. In a rare show of informality, Bacca had unbuttoned his suit jacket and loosened the knot on his necktie.

Bacca was the most famous crafter in the entire Overworld. He was known far and wide for remarkable feats of crafting, and equally impressive accomplishments of bravery and guile. His creations were famous for their beauty, for their usefulness, and for being generally awesome.

Bacca himself was about the same size as most other crafters, but in all other ways his appearance was very different. Every inch of Bacca was covered with short fur, making him look a little bit like a dog or a wolf, or maybe even a particularly well-groomed bear. He had very long canine teeth and his nose was suspiciously close to a snout. But despite this animal hairiness, Bacca managed a very formal appearance. He always kept his fur cleaned and combed, and never went anywhere without his trademark three-piece suit.

Bacca's castle was perhaps his finest crafting creation of all. It was perched dramatically on the edge of a cliff and featured some of the tallest towers and spires in all the Minecraft universe. On the lawns in front of his castle, Bacca had crafted expansive gardens filled with blue orchids, tulips, and sunflowers. Crafters came from all around the Overworld to see Bacca's impressive home and marvel at these gardens. Bacca didn't mind the visitors. He was friendly, and liked guests. Sometimes, he even invited them to come inside and enjoy some raw fish, which was his favorite food—and, in fact, the only food he ate. Luckily for Bacca, being the top crafter around came with plenty of benefits. Being able to craft enormous fish tanks with endless supplies of yummy fish was just one of them!

Although Bacca could often be sassy and sarcastic, he was kind and cared about other people. At his core, the most important thing for Bacca was helping others. It wasn't enough for Bacca just to challenge himself to make bigger and better crafting creations—though he certainly did that. It was also important to Bacca to be a mentor to the next generation of crafters. Which was why, every summer, he took time out of his busy crafting schedule to host a special workshop for the Overworld's leading young crafters.

And today, because it was such a nice day, Bacca had decided that they could have class outside.

Seated in a half circle around Bacca were ten very gifted young crafters. Most of them were not old enough to be on their own yet, and had to be dropped off by their parents. In most cases, Overworld parents were delighted when their child was selected for Bacca's yearly master class. (Successful graduates were presented with the prestigious "Baccalaureate" degree, which came with a diploma and a set of fine crafting tools. It virtually guaranteed a long and prosperous career in crafting. Suffice it to say, the class had a very competitive application process.)

Assisting Bacca with the teaching was Bacca's girlfriend, LadyBacc. An accomplished crafter in her own right, LadyBacc was perhaps the perfect match for Bacca. She looked more or less exactly like him—which could sometimes be hilarious and confusing—except that she wore a dress instead of a suit, and had a ribbon tied to her mane. Both Bacca and LadyBacc loved being sarcastic and silly, but when it came to crafting they were both dead-serious.

This year, their summer crafting class had turned out to be unexpectedly controversial. That was because, for the first time, a zombie had been admitted.

The zombie's name was Dug. (Not "Doug" as Bacca had originally thought, but "Dug," as the young crafter's parents had carefully explained. It had to do with digging . . . like out of a grave . . . because you were a member of the walking dead!)

Many people in the Overworld disliked zombies, and this was true of most of the parents of the crafters in Bacca's class. When they'd dropped their sons and daughters off, some of them had let Bacca know exactly how they felt.

"So a zombie's in your class this year?" one of the parents had said rather rudely. "I guess it's not as exclusive as we thought."

"You're letting a *zombie* crafter in?" another parent had quipped. "What's next? Sheep crafters? Pig crafters? What about very smart mushrooms?"

"I've got *nothing* against zombies," said still another parent. "I like them just fine. When they're lurking in the shadows and trying to eat people. You know, like zombies are *supposed* to. But a zombie trying to be a *crafter*? That's just too strange!"

Other parents had expressed concern about the safety of their children around a zombie. Bacca knew that this was silly, if only because he would be present at all times, and could easily put a stop to any roughhousing. (In addition to being a renowned crafter, Bacca was also a highly skilled warrior. He never went anywhere without his diamond axe, which he had lovingly named Betty. Breaking up fights between students, even zombie ones, would be no problem for him.)

For his part, Bacca was actually excited about his zombie student. This was because Dug was one of the fastest learners of any crafter Bacca had ever met. Period. While his style was sometimes a little rough around the edges—mostly owing to the lousy selection of crafting tools available to zombies—Dug showed enormous potential. Who knew what he might be able to accomplish with a little bit of guidance?

The undead didn't have parents in the same way that living crafters did, but it was clear that a group of zombies had claimed Dug as their own. These zombies showed up to drop off Dug on the first day of class, right at the momentt before night became morning. (Most zombies had to stay underground during the day because they burned in sunlight. Baby zombies did not burn, however, and were effectively sun proof. Dug wasn't a baby, but he wasn't an adult either. As near as Bacca could tell, the sun didn't hurt Dug yet, but he still preferred to be in the shade whenever possible.) Bacca had made a point to have a friendly chat with Dug's parents. He could see in the rotting, half-formed faces of these zombies that they were incredibly proud of their young protégé.

On this particular morning, the class was learning to craft golden chestplates. The task involved smelting gold ore into gold ingots, and then using eight of the ingots to carefully create the finished piece of armor. It was only their first day working with gold, but Bacca was already seeing a lot of advanced work from his students.

"That's some nice hammering, Jason," Bacca said as he strode from crafter to crafter, reviewing each student's progress. "Make sure you get the front of the breastplate nice and smooth, but don't make it too thin. Remember, this thing has got to protect somebody from a creeper or a skeleton or a z—"

Bacca stopped himself, remembering his new student."

"Or a . . . ?" said the student, waiting for him to finish.

"Or a zebra, I was going to say," Bacca lied. "They can, you know, run up and kick you when you're not looking. It's very unpleasant."

Bacca quickly moved down the row of crafters.

"That's looking excellent, Sara," Bacca said to the next pupil. "Be sure to reinforce the top so that it protects the wearer's shoulders."

"Will do!" said the enthusiastic student.

Then Bacca arrived at the crafting table where Dug was working. The young zombie did not appear to be in very much of a hurry. Maybe Dug was lazy? Bacca knew that zombies tended to move slowly, and so he was prepared to give his student the benefit of the doubt. However, after a moment, Bacca realized that the lack of action was due to the fact that Dug was already finished.

"Let's see what you've got here," Bacca said, picking up the gold chestplate and turning it over.

It was immaculate. Strong and lightweight, the front of the armor had been polished to a brilliant golden gleam. The young crafter had even adorned it with tasteful engravings along the edges. Looking more closely, Bacca saw that they were engravings of zombies.

This kid is ready to work with diamond, Bacca thought to himself. Dug was already head and shoulders above the other crafters in the class. Higher than that. He was practically up in his own stratosphere.

"Very nice work," Bacca said evenly.

Bacca hesitated to tell the young zombie just how skilled he actually was. Bacca didn't want the other crafters in the class to get jealous. He also didn't want Dug to grow an inflated ego.

"Mmmm," Dug responded with a smile. Traditional speech was a challenge for zombies. They could talk, but they preferred simply to moan whenever that would get the point across. Dug was no exception.

With his single moan, Dug seemed to transmit the idea that Bacca didn't have to worry, because while Dug might have been many things—like, say, a living corpse reanimated to feast on crafters—'intimiated' wasn't one of them.

Bacca liked this boldness, and gave his student a grin. Then he stepped over to where LadyBacc was preparing the next lesson—a lecture on bone meal and its many useful properties.

"This zombie kid is just blowing everybody away," Bacca whispered. "I'm really impressed."

"I know," agreed LadyBacc. "So am I. Did you see the iron sword he crafted on the very first day?"

"I sure did," Bacca replied. "He made the cross guard and hilt without even being told how. And that blade! It was practically sharp enough to split obsidian."

"Can you believe there were people who thought Dug shouldn't even be here?" asked LadyBacc.

"I think those skeptics are going to come around soon," Bacca said confidently. "Especially when they see what hecan do."

"And he hasn't tried to bite any of the other students even once," she observed.

"Yes," he replied. "That's a point in his favor as well."

"But back to his crafting, I think he's ready for diamond."

"I was just thinking that myself," Bacca told her. "This afternoon, maybe one of us should show him how to . . . how to . . ."

Bacca trailed off. He seemed to have lost his train of thought. He was looking past LadyBacc and squinting into the distance.

LadyBacc was confused. She turned around and followed Bacca's gaze.

On the horizon, a distant crowd of people, maybe twenty or thirty of them, was approaching the castle. They were crafters, she realized—some of whom Bacca and LadyBacc had met before—and they looked *very unhappy*.

"Uh oh," LadyBacc said. "Do you think they're here about Dug? Should we move the children inside?"

"No, I'm going to give them the benefit of the doubt," Bacca said cautiously. "They're mad about *something*, but it's not like they're holding torches and pitchforks. Besides, I know some of these crafters personally. They're not people who get angry over something like a zombie student. Can you watch the students for a bit? I'm going to go hear what they have to say."

Bacca walked across his front lawn to meet the approaching mob. As they drew closer, Bacca began to think they looked less hostile, and more like they might just need help. More than one of the crafters had dusty clothes and faces covered in dirt. A few of them were missing shoes, making Bacca think they'd been running away from something.

"Hi everybody!" Bacca said as the mob drew close. "Why the long faces? What's going on?"

"Oh Bacca," said a spokesman from the group. "We're here to seek your assistance!"

The spokesman was a talented smelter named Brian. Bacca had met him a time or two before, and admired his fine ingots. Bacca knew that Brian was very shy, and liked to live a quiet life away from crowds. If Brian had joined up with a big group like this, then Bacca guessed it was for a very important reason.

"Tell me the details," Bacca said. "Why do you need my help?"

"It's the zombies and the skeletons!" Brian said. The rest of the crowd behind him nodded seriously in agreement.

"What about them?" Bacca said, thinking maybe he'd been wrong and bracing himself for something about how his zombie student was taking a spot at the school away from other crafters.

Instead, Brian said: "They're acting all wrong. They're violent. It's like they've gone crazy."

Bacca wrinkled his nose to show he didn't understand.

"But being violent is what mobs do," he said. "And skeletons and zombies are mobs, so . . . ?"

"Hang on," Brian said. "There's more to it. They're not just being violent . . . they're being violent with *each other*."

"You mean to say that zombies and skeletons are . . . fighting?" Bacca asked.

The entire crowd of crafters nodded yes.

"And it's not just a few of 'em . . . it's *all* of 'em!" someone shouted from the back.

"Yeah," shouted someone else. "They're joining up into great big armies, and then charging right into each other!"

Armies of zombies and skeletons? Bacca had never heard of such a thing. It was true that members of different mobs sometimes fought with each other—a zombie fighting a skeleton was not unheard of, for example—but it was usually an isolated incident. It typically happened by sheer accident. (Bacca usually thought it was fun when it did. You could take bets on which mob member you thought was going to win.) Certainly, zombies had never been known to go *in search of* skeletons, or vice versa. But these crafters seemed to be saying that that had changed.

"How long has this been going on?" Bacca asked.

"Just for a few days," Brian answered. "But it's already a big problem! When they fight each other, they mess up all the stuff we built."

"It's true!" shouted another crafter. "Yesterday a zombie army marched across my farm. They trampled all my crops, and knocked down all of my buildings. On top of that, my animals ran away!"

"The skeletons are just as bad," said another crafter. "A bunch of them walked through my fountains and pools that had taken me months to build. They pushed over the statues, and displaced all the water. Worst of all, they stepped on my fish!"

"Poor fish," someone said from the back of the group. "They hadn't done anything to anyone . . . they were just swimming around."

Bacca frowned sympathetically. The unnecessary wasting of delicious fish was something that struck a chord with him.

"And I used to live next to a beautiful valley," Brian said. "That was the whole reason I built my house there. Location, location, location. Well, now my location is ruined! The other night an army of zombies and an army of skeletons showed up at the same time. They charged into the valley and fought each other for hours. I don't know who won, but now my valley is a giant pit of mud filled with armor and arrows and dead skeletons and zombies."

"Erm . . ." someone said from the back of the group. "But I thought skeletons and zombies were *technically* already dead, so—"

"You know what I mean!" snapped Brian. He was clearly in a lousy mood.

"This does sound like a serious problem," Bacca said.

"You're the most famous crafter and the bravest warrior in the entire Overworld," Brian said to Bacca. "So we're coming to you in hopes that you can fix things. Somehow, we need to make the skeletons and the zombies stop fighting. It's making everything awful for everybody."

Bacca rubbed his hairy chin and considered carefully. He wanted to help the crafters if he could, but this request was so unusual. He had never heard anything like it. Bacca was certainly skilled at combat himself. If the request had been to take on a zombie army or a skeleton army—or both!—Bacca would have been up for it . . . and then some! (It might have been fun to make a game of it, and see which army he could defeat more quickly. For a moment, Bacca mentally explored the fun possibilities.) But to make two mobs stop fighting with *each other*? This was a completely different kettle of fish!

"Do any of you know *why* the zombies and the skeletons are fighting?" Bacca asked. "Has there been an argument? Did one group insult the other?"

"We don't know," Brian said. "Nobody does. Maybe they've *always* hated each other . . . and only now gotten around to fighting about it."

Bacca rubbed his chin again. That sure didn't sound right. Wars didn't start for no reason. If these two mobs were at each other's throats (or neckbones, in the skeletons' case), something new had probably happened. Something bad.

"Okay," said Bacca. "I'll investigate. But I can't make any promises."

"Thank you," several crafters said at once.

"Yes, thank you," Brian added. "That's all we ask."

Pleased to know that Bacca was on the case, the group of crafters in front of his castle gradually began to disperse. Bacca strode back to where his crafting class was still in session. Many of the young crafters had seen the commotion and wondered what was going on. LadyBacc was also curious about what the visitors had wanted.

"Have you heard anything about zombies and skeletons fighting?" Bacca asked his girlfriend.

"Not more than usual," she said. "Usually, I'm more concerned with how *I* can fight *them*."

"Apparently big groups of zombies and skeletons are going to war," Bacca said. "It's causing a lot of problems. The crafters are really upset. They want me to help."

"Help how?" asked LadyBacc.

"I'm not quite sure yet," Bacca answered.

"Well, if anyone can get to the bottom of this, it's you," LadyBacc said, giving her boyfriend a vote of confidence.

"I guess so," Bacca said. "I expect this will take a while to investigate. Do you mind teaching the class until I get back? You're every bit the crafter I am. Plus, all the students love you."

"Sure thing," said LadyBacc. She then smiled slyly. "On one condition."

"What's that?" asked Bacca.

"Take Dug with you."

Of all the possible conditions, Bacca was not expecting that one.

"What?" he replied. "Why in the Overworld should I do that?"

"I'll give you three reasons," LadyBacc said confidently. "For one, there's almost nothing we can teach him. You know that. He's the best young crafter we've ever seen. He already knows almost everything, and anything that *is* new he picks up instantly. Taking him with you for a few days might give the others in the class a chance to catch up!

"For another, he's a zombie. That might be useful. If something is going on with the zombies and the skeletons, it might help to have a zombie on your team.

"And finally, I'm sure it would mean a lot to him. I know he doesn't say much, but Dug tends to moan in a special, more enthusiastic way when he gets some praise from you. Helping you with a quest would be the highlight of his summer!"

"Hmm, you make some good points," Bacca said, looking over to the workbench where Dug was lovingly polishing his gold breastplate. "As you know, eventually all crafters have to learn that crafting is about more than just making items or building blocks in a workshop. It's about interacting with the environment of the Overworld around you. It's about building structures that complement their surroundings, and using the natural landscape as an asset instead of a hindrance. I guess taking Dug out into the larger world might introduce him to some of these ideas."

"See?" said LadyBacc. "I knew you'd come around."

"But I'll only take him if he wants to go," Bacca quickly added. "Nothing would be worse than dragging a complaining zombie with me the whole way."

Bacca stepped over to where Dug was polishing the breastplate. With a tip of his head, Bacca silently indicated that the zombie should follow him. Bacca strode a few paces away, to where the other students would not be able to hear. Dug put down his breastplate and enthusiastically loped after him.

"So, Dug . . ." he began when the zombie caught up. "Something important is happening, and it looks like I have to go away for a while on a mission of special importance."

Dug looked sad. His face fell. Literally. The skin on Dug's face was not attached very tightly. (Being a zombie will do that to you. Dug's nose and mouth dropped perhaps a full inch lower on Bacca's bad news.)

"It's going to involve a lot of travel and it might be dangerous," Bacca continued. "All the same . . . I thought you might like to come with me."

"Mmmm!" Dug said. He nodded enthusiastically, and his face snapped back into place.

"We would need to leave right away, and I'm not sure when we'll be back," Bacca cautioned. "You're sure about this? You really want to come?"

"mmmm Yes," Dug managed, giving another nod.

"Okay then," Bacca said. "Get your things packed into your inventory, and I'll go do the same. We'll depart in a few minutes."

Bacca returned to LadyBacc.

"Looks like he's in," Bacca said. "Just promise me this is a good idea."

"I promise you," LadyBacc said. "It's a *very* good idea. Great, in fact. It might be the best we've ever had."

"OK," said Bacca. "I'm holding you to that."

Bacca went inside his castle and filled his inventory full of supplies for the journey ahead. Of course, the most important thing in Bacca's inventory was his diamond axe Betty. He never went anywhere without it. In addition to Betty, Bacca packed armor, crafting materials, and valuable blocks he could use as money if the need arose. He also packed exotic crafting blocks that might be hard to find out in the wild. Instead of food, Bacca grabbed his favorite fishing rod which featured a very effective Lure enchantment—he would catch his dinner whenever he got hungry. (For a moment, Bacca wondered about what Dug would eat. Then Bacca remembered exactly what zombies ate, and decided it might be better not to think about it.)

By the time Bacca stepped back outside, Dug was ready to go. The other students craned their necks to see what was happening. They could tell that something was afoot.

"Where are you going to start?" LadyBacc asked Bacca. She gave him a kiss goodbye on his hairy cheek.

"I want to see what these crafters are talking about," Bacca replied. "That guy Brian, who was leading the group, said there was a big zombies-versus-skeletons battle right beside his house. I'd like to see that battlefield with my own eyes. I might find some clues that Brian and the other crafters missed."

"Do you think the crafters could be exaggerating the size of the mobs?" LadyBacc asked. "People like to exaggerate sometimes. Could there really be entire zombie and skeleton *armies*?"

"I won't know for sure until I see for myself," Bacca said. "Dug, are you ready to go?"

The zombie nodded enthusiastically and managed another: "mmmm*Yes.*"

Bacca turned to the other crafting students.

"Okay, listen up," Bacca said. "Dug and I have to go away for a while. Something's happening and our help is needed."

There were groans of disappointment.

"But don't worry," Bacca said. "While I'm away, LadyBacc will be taking over all the classes. She's an Overworld-class crafter. At least as good as I am."

Bacca gave his girlfriend a wink.

All of the students had to nod in agreement. There wasn't a single one who didn't know this to be absolutely true.

"Okay then," Bacca said. "We should get started. It's a long walk to Brian's place."

"Be sure to be careful," LadyBacc said, waving goodbye.

"I always am," Bacca replied.

As Bacca and Dug turned to go, one of the students called after them.

"But Mister Bacca, sir," the student said. "What exactly *is* happening?"

"That," said Bacca, "is precisely what I'm going to find out."

CHAPTER THREE

Bacca and Dug journeyed across the beautiful Overworld together. Like most zombies, Dug tended toward the quieter side, but was not entirely silent. Sometimes when they passed an interesting feature in the landscape, Dug would point it out. Other times, he would note the crafting materials that could be derived from a particular material growing around them. A sandy beach got Dug very excited about all the glass that could be crafted. A mountain in the distance with exposed chunks of cobblestone prompted him to expound on all the fine stone blocks it could make. (In Dug's case, "expound" meant using more than ten words.) Bacca marveled time and again at his student's knowledge and enthusiasm. Zombie or not, he was clearly far ahead of all of his peers—and most adult crafters too! Bacca knew the future would hold big things for the little crafter.

When it seemed like they had been walking forever, with no end in sight, the hilly region where Brian lived finally came into view. As they grew closer, Bacca noticed a strange scent on the wind. It smelled a lot like bodies that had been underground for a long time. And then reanimated.

Dug sniffed at the air.

"You smell that too?" Bacca asked.

Dug nodded.

"mmmm*Zombies*," he said. "mmmm*Not* just me. Lots and lots of them."

Crossing over the lip of a hillside, they suddenly stood before a great swath of destruction that had been cut through the green floor of the valley. Hundreds or thousands of zombies had walked through here, Bacca realized. They had trampled down the grass, and knocked over anything that stood in their way. They had also left behind telltale zombie signs, like bits of torn clothing, pieces of rusty iron armor, and sometimes even rotted-off fingers and toes. (Zombies were always falling apart.)

Bacca looked down at Dug, who nodded seriously. They were on the right path.

"I've never seen anything like this," Bacca said. "I didn't think there were enough zombies on this entire server plane to do this much damage!"

"mmmm*More* of us than you think," replied Dug.

"Yeah, I guess so," quipped Bacca.

Bacca and Dug followed the path of destruction. Just as Bacca had suspected it would, the path led right to the house of Brian the smelter. There was smoke coming from his chimney, indicating that he was already back home and hard at work. It was impossible for Bacca to smell the smoke that came from the chimney, however—even with his fantastic, nearly-canine sense of smell—because the odor of zombies and skeletons overpowered everything else.

"I have a feeling you can guess what's on the other side of that hill," Bacca said. "If you don't think you can handle it, you don't have to come with me."

Dug did not slow his gait.

"mmmm*Important*," Dug said. "My people. I need to see."

"Okay," said Bacca. "But I think it's going to be pretty gross."

It was.

As they reached the top of the hill and looked down into the valley, they saw a landscape filled with the bodies of skeletons and zombies. They had quite evidently been fighting each other. The zombies were full of arrows from skeleton bows, and the skeletons' bones were covered in zombie bites. The valley floor was covered in rotten flesh dropped by dead zombies, and bones and arrows dropped by the skeletons. It wasn't clear if there had even been a winner. Both armies seemed to have lost an equal number of soldiers. If there had been any survivors, they had long since wandered away.

"Caught one of them, have you?"

Bacca and Dug turned around to see that Brian had emerged from his house. He was pointing at Dug.

"No, no, no," Bacca said. "Dug is not one of 'them.' He's my student. He's helping me."

"A zombie student?" Brian said skeptically.

"That's right," Bacca said. "I'm teaching him to craft."

"A zombie *crafter*?" Brian said even more skeptically.

"A zombie crafter who's better than most crafters on this server plane," Bacca said. "And not just for his age. This morning I saw him make a gold breastplate that could stop an arrow shot by a giant. And he did it in about ten minutes. How many gold breastplates have *you* crafted recently?"

Bacca didn't like bragging about Dug—especially in front of Dug—but Brian needed to be set straight.

"Um . . . uh . . ." Brian stammered. "I'm really more of a smelter, actually. Not so into crafting breastplates."

"That's what I thought," said Bacca with a grin.

There was a rustling sound a few feet away. Bacca and Brian turned to see that Dug had crept down into the valley and was inspecting the pile of undead bodies. Several of the zombies had worn armor, but most of it was rusty and not very good. Bacca wondered if the zombies might have won if they'd had a crafter like Dug to supply them with better equipment. *Wait a second,* Bacca reminded himself, shaking his furry head. *The point of his mission was to stop the fighting!*

Bacca decided to think along different lines.

Dug picked up a severed zombie arm that still clutched an iron sword.

"Was it anybody that you knew?" Brian asked.

Bacca frowned, thinking that his question was rather insensitive, considering the circumstances.

"mmmm*Gravehome*," Dug moaned.

"That zombie's name was 'Gravehome'?" Brian asked. "How can you tell from just an arm?"

"Gravehome's not a zombie; it's a place," Bacca corrected him. "It's a mountain fortress in the middle of an ice plains spikes biome. It's way up north. To get there, you have to cross a bunch of packed ice and snow. Then you suddenly see this mountain covered in graves. I've only been there once. Apparently, some sort of zombie king lives inside. I've never met him."

Bacca turned to Dug, who was still inspecting the arm.

"Dug, are you saying that these zombies came from Gravehome?"

Dug slowly nodded yes. He pointed to a distinct engraving on the iron sword's blade.

"mmmm*Gravehome* sword," Dug said.

"I wonder why zombies would come all the way from Gravehome to fight skeletons out here," Bacca said.

The young zombie shrugged.

"I've heard that the zombies in Gravehome serve a kind of zombie king," Bacca continued. "Is that true, Dug?"

"mmmm*Yes*," Dug said. "All zombies serve him."

"Then this didn't happen by accident," Bacca said. "The Zombie King must have ordered this army to fight the skeletons."

"But why would they fight here?" Brian asked. "My little valley isn't important to anyone but me. Why would zombies want it? Or skeletons, for that matter?"

"I'm wondering the same thing," Bacca told him.

Dug put down the zombie arm and began sifting through some nearby skeleton bones. They were obviously not familiar to him. He held the glistening white objects up to the sunlight, studying them, trying to learn anything he could.

"What about the skeletons?" Brian called. "Do *they* have a king?"

"Actually, they do," Bacca said. "But I've never met him, either."

"Somebody should go talk to them," Brian said, nervously wringing his hands. "Find out why they're so mad at each other."

Bacca smiled.

"That's not a bad idea," Bacca said.

Dug waded back up out of the morass of dead zombies and skeletons.

"What do you think?" Bacca said to him. "Should we go have a few words with your king?"

Dug nodded.

"And tell that Zombie King that next time his zombies have a battle, it's shouldn't be in my valley," added Brian. "My beautiful view is ruined!"

"I'll be sure to pass that along," Bacca said, rolling his eyes.

Dug and Bacca left the valley and turned north. They walked through many different biomes until they reached one that was full of ice and snow. The rivers running through this biome froze solid. The ground was covered with snow and had packed ice underneath. The trees were also covered with snow. Before long, the packed ice began jutting up out of the ground, forming giant spikes.

"See those?" Bacca said, pointing to the spikes. "It means we're getting close."

"Mmmm," agreed Dug. "Also getting cold."

Bacca reflected on the benefits of his having a natural fur coat at all times. It could be unpleasant in the heat of a desert, but in an icy landscape it certainly came in handy.

In the far distance, the outline of a mountain became visible. It was so tall that it seemed to touch the clouds. Protruding from the surface of the mountain were thousands and thousands of small constructions. As Bacca and Dug got closer, they could see these constructions for what they really were. Headstones. Grave markers. The mountain was completely covered with them.

Bacca and Dug headed straight for it.

Inside of Gravehome, the Zombie King tried to relax.

Located deep within the mountain, his throne room had been carved out of blocks of stone and coated in a layer of dirt. There were blocks of grass too, but instead of covering the floor, they were hanging down from the ceiling so the king could look up at them—much as a zombie waiting to pop out of the ground might anticipate the grassy lawn above him. It was also very dark. The overall effect of the architecture was profoundly grave-ey. This pleased the zombies very much.

Arrayed in front of the Zombie King were various members of his court. Important zombie statesmen, generals, and diplomats were seated at tables. His most trusted advisors were positioned directly next to his throne. The throne itself was very impressive looking; made entirely of the darkest blocks of obsidian, and with a tall back that rose several feet above the king's head.

The Zombie King anxiously drummed the three remaining fingers of his right hand on the armrest. Despite the finery around him, the king was uneasy. He had a problem. A very *big* problem. One that he hoped would be solved soon.

The king perked up when a zombie messenger shuffled into the throne room. All heads (slowly) turned to see what he had to say. The Zombie King's remaining eyebrow lifted expectantly.

While zombies have difficulty turning their moans into speech that can be understood by humans, they can communicate quite quickly *via* moans when talking to other zombies. The zombie moan vocabulary is full of interesting words with complicated meanings. (Some cultures had twenty different words for 'snow.' Zombies had twenty moans for rotten flesh, and about fifty for iron swords and pumpkins.) Unfortunately for humans, only other zombies can understand this rich and varied language.

What is the news? the Zombie King asked with a moan. *Are our armies victorious? Have we retrieved that which the skeletons have taken? Please tell me!*

No, my liege, the messenger moaned back. *I have other information. A hairy crafter named 'Bacca' is here to see you. He says it's important.*

The king sat back, disappointed.

I don't have time for hairy crafters, the king moaned. *Especially not when my kingdom is in crisis. Send him away.*

My liege, he is not alone, the messenger continued. *There is a young zombie with him.*

A zombie prisoner, you say? asked the king, suddenly outraged. *I do not negotiate with kidnappers! Give me a sword! I will defeat him in battle myself, and free this zombie.*

No, said the messenger. *Nothing like that. The zombie is not a prisoner. The zombie is also a crafter. The hairy one is apparently his . . . teacher.*

This is very strange, the king moaned thoughtfully. *Very well. I will receive them.*

The Zombie King watched the messenger hurry out of the throne room to fetch the visitors.

These were very strange times, the king thought to himself. His people at war. A national crisis looming. Pressure on the throne from every direction.

In strange times, you never knew what was going to make the difference between success or failure. A hairy crafter and a zombie crafter might not be important . . . but on the other hand, they might be *very* important. Either way, it felt too unusual to ignore.

Be careful my liege.

This voice came from Drooler, the king's most-trusted advisor. Drooler sat closest to the king's throne. He was an ancient zombie who wore the only complete set of diamond armor in Gravehome.

The king slowly turned to look at his bejeweled advisor.

These two could be assassins, sent by the skeletons, warned Drooler. *We don't know them. For your own safety, let me and some guards deal with them instead.*

Just because we are in an emergency, does not mean we should be afraid of every little thing, the Zombie King replied. *I appreciate your concern for my safety, Drooler. However, as the king of my people, I shouldn't hide behind others. I should lead and be brave.*

Drooler opened his mouth to object again, but it was too late. Loud footsteps sounded just outside the throne room. At least one set of them sounded like *hairy* footsteps. The king prepared to receive his mystery guests.

Bacca had never seen so many zombies before. And that included the valley full of dead ones he'd just left behind.

Gravehome was *filled* with zombies. There were zombies of every size and shape. Tall ones and short ones. Fat ones and thin ones. Some could have almost passed for living crafters, while some were so decrepit that they were little more than skeletons themselves. All of them were turning (or had already turned) some variety of dark green. They looked at Bacca and Dug with great suspicion as the pair hurried past, following their zombie guide.

Eventually, the guide stopped in front of a high archway made entirely of thick blocks of bedrock. Bacca could see that on the other side was a room full of important-looking zombies. Oddly, the room had a ceiling made entirely of grass.

"mmmm*Throne* room," the zombie attendant managed. "King's in here."

Then, the zombie moaned just to Dug: *I don't know what you and your hairy friend are up to, but you better not waste the king's time.*

Dug didn't know what to say, so he just nodded. Then they passed through the archway and entered the room.

There were many zombies inside, but it was easy to locate the king. He was sitting on a high-backed throne and wore a crown of mummified flesh. He appeared to be chatting with a zombie in glistening diamond armor.

The zombies stood up and watched as Bacca and Dug slowly approached the king. Some of the zombies held weapons. Clearly, they were ready to protect the king if he was threatened.

"Hello," said Bacca.

The Zombie King moaned in greeting.

"I'm Bacca, and this is my friend Dug," he continued confidently. "We're here because . . . well, the other crafters and I, we've been seeing great big zombie armies marching around. This concerns us because these armies have been destroying a lot of our carefully crafted creations. They've been knocking over buildings. Trampling topiary. Mucking-up landscaping. You name it, it's being demolished."

The king looked back and forth between Bacca and Dug. He did not seem to grasp the seriousness of the problem.

"So, we were wondering," Bacca continued. "Is there any chance that this could, you know, *stop*? And soon?"

The zombie king began to moan a reply.

"mmmm*Bacca*. Yes. Come to think of it, I have heard of you. Powerful crafter, they say."

"Yeah, I can do some stuff," Bacca said with a wry smile.

"mmmm*You* will make a *zombie* crafter?" the king asked, gesturing to Dug.

"He's more or less already made," Bacca answered. "The first day at my workshop he was doing things that many crafters need a lifetime to learn. The kid's a natural. He's born to do it. Born . . . or, you know . . . whatever zombies are."

The king looked guarded and cautious.

"mmmm*Not* sure that I agree with zombies crafting," he said. "I think it is a controversial idea."

"You and half the crafters on the Overworld," Bacca replied with a chuckle. "Some people don't want zombies to try new things. But I say if a zombie wants to be a crafter, he should go for it!"

The king nodded to say he appreciated Bacca's point of view, even if he didn't agree with it.

"mmmm*But* as to your request," the Zombie King said, "that, I cannot grant. For we are at war."

"I kinda guessed that much," Bacca said. "But why are you at war with the skeletons? What'd they do?"

The king and his advisors exchanged an uneasy glance. Then they began moaning. It was a series of long, high-pitched moans—that seemed to both pose and answer questions. Bacca realized it was a conversion. One that left him out on purpose.

"Pssst, what's going on?" he whispered to Dug.

"mmmm*Arguing*," Dug whispered back.

"Over what?"

"mmmm*Over* whether they should trust us," Dug said.

No sooner were these words out of Dug's mouth, than the Zombie King slammed his fist down hard on the armrest of his throne. The blow was so powerful that one of his dried-up fingertips broke off and skittered across the floor, landing at Bacca's foot. The moaning fell silent. The king had clearly made his decision.

Bacca looked down at the fingertip, then back up at the king, wondering if it would be polite to pick it up and return it.

"mmmm*My* trusted counselor Drooler disagrees, but I think you are worthy of the truth," the king said slowly.

The zombie in the diamond armor shook his head. He obviously thought the king was making a bad decision.

"mmmm*Our* armies are at war with the skeletons because they have stolen the Bonesword," the king said.

Bacca heard Dug gasp. (Having several holes in different parts of his undead chest, this made Dug sound a little bit like a dropped accordion.)

Bacca knew of the Bonesword, but only vaguely. He'd heard it was a ceremonial item zombies used when there was a new king or queen. It supposedly wasn't magic—or even particularly sharp—but its sentimental meaning was apparently enormous. It was engraved with important scenes from zombie history. There were also weird, old prophecies surrounding it. But Bacca's ancient zombie history wasn't what it used to be (and to be clear, practically *all* zombie history was ancient), and he frowned, straining to remember more details.

"mmmm*I* see from your expression that you understand how grave a situation this is," the Zombie King said.

"Sort of," Bacca answered. "I know you use the Bonesword to swear-in new zombie kings and queens, right? And there's supposed to be old prophecies about it. I think one says that if it's lost, the king or queen in power has to step down. Is that correct? I can see how that would be a problem for you."

The zombie on the throne gave an almost imperceptible nod.

"But you're still king, right?" Bacca pressed.

"mmmm*It* is our custom that if the Bonesword were to be lost, the ruler must leave the throne," said the king. "That much is correct. But what is 'lost?' Our experts on zombie scripture tell me that the Bonesword is not truly lost if we know where it is. And we know where it is."

"You do?" asked Bacca.

The king nodded.

Suddenly, Drooler, the king's counselor, began to speak. His voice was high pitched and squeaky, and not nearly as pleasant as the king's.

"mmmm*Of* course we know where it is," Drooler said aggressively. "The skeletons have it. They have taken it to their temple in the jungle biome!"

The king nodded.

"mmmm*And* as long as we know where it is, it is not truly lost," added the Zombie King. "I am assured that I have the authority to remain king during its . . . mmmm*temporary* absence. But we must have it back as soon as possible."

"I still have a lot of questions," Bacca said. "When did they take it? Why would they want it? With all respect, the Bonesword isn't magic or anything, right? It's just a long, sharp bone."

"mmmm*We* saw them take it," the king said. "Drooler was an eyewitness."

The zombie in the diamond armor nodded proudly.

"mmmm*The* Bonesword is kept on a polished granite platform surrounded by blocks of gold and blocks of emerald—deep inside a special ceremonial chamber," explained Drooler. "Torches light it beautifully from below. Pressure plates surround it for security purposes. Armored zombies stand watch all day and night."

"Sounds pretty safe to me," Bacca said, wondering how the sword could have been taken under such close watch.

"mmmm*Two* weeks ago, I went to the ceremonial chamber late at night to check on it. Only the guards had disappeared, and a big group of skeletons was inside. They tied me up and took the Bonesword. Then they crawled out through the ceiling using a rope, and pulled the rope up after them. I tried to moan for help, but they also tied my mouth shut. It was hours before anyone found me."

"Gee, that sounds like some professional skeleton crooks," Bacca said cautiously. He was not sure he believed Drooler's story.

"mmmm*As* to the question of *why* they would want it, I can answer that," said the Zombie King.

"Skeletons have *always* been envious of zombies. It shouldn't be surprising if you think about it. We can wear armor. We use weapons other than bows. We have flesh left on our bones—at least most of us do. And we emit loud, awesome-sounding moans. Why *wouldn't* they be jealous? Why *wouldn't* they want to steal our favorite things?"

"So they took the Bonesword out of jealously?" said Bacca. Secretly, he was not convinced; so far, the zombies' story was not really adding up.

Skeletons were not any brighter than zombies, but Bacca knew that even *they* should have seen that taking the Bonesword would start a war. It didn't make any sense. There had to be some important information still missing.

"mmmm*So* you see," continued the Zombie King, "we must march into skeleton territory, defeat them, and take back the Bonesword. It will be returned to its rightful place, and I will remain king."

"There's nothing I can say to convince you to stop fighting?" Bacca asked.

"mmmm*No!*" Drooler barked loudly. "We will muster bigger and bigger armies. We will fight the skeletons wherever we find them, until the sword is ours. If some silly crafters have their creations destroyed in the process, then so what?"

Bacca thought carefully about what to say next. Tensions were high. There had to be a way to keep this from escalating. If Bacca did nothing, much of the Overworld could be destroyed by the skeletons and zombies fighting. The crafters had come to Bacca for help, and the war was only two weeks old. What would the Overworld look like if this lasted for months? Or years?

"I have an idea," said Bacca. "What if *I* get the Bonesword back for you?"

The zombies looked at one another skeptically.

"mmmm*A* crafter—even a very famous one—cannot succeed where whole armies have failed," insisted Drooler. "You must be as crazy as you are hairy."

Bacca ignored this thinly-veiled jab—he was *proud* of being hairy!—and spoke to the Zombie King directly.

"I'll make a deal with you. Call off your armies for just one week, and I'll get the Bonesword back for you. Just seven days. That's all I need."

Drooler opened his mouth to object, but the king was already intrigued.

"mmmm*How* will you do this?" the king asked.

"First, I'll go and talk to the skeletons," Bacca said. "I can be very convincing. If they don't want to give it back, then I'll try something else. What have you got to lose, except more soldiers?"

The Zombie King drummed his remaining fingers. He appeared to be considering it.

"mmmm*My* liege . . ." objected Drooler. "You're not seriously going to let this lowly crafter interrupt our glorious and noble war, are you?"

The king turned to Drooler and stared him down. He had made his decision.

"mmmm*Very* well, Bacca," said the Zombie King. "I am going to call your bluff. I have heard you can be a useful man. But I am going to make an addition to our bargain. Your student, Dug . . . this question of whether or not he should be a crafter intrigues me. If you show me that two crafters can return our Bonesword safely, then Dug may continue his studies with my blessings. But if you fail, then Dug must renounce crafting forever and enlist in the zombie army, where it seems to me that a zombie like him would be best suited. What do you say to that?"

Bacca's jaw dropped. He had not been expecting this. He was fairly confident he could find a way to get the Bonesword back, but he was not about to wager a young crafter's future on it.

Bacca started to tell the Zombie King that this was asking too much, and that it wasn't fair to put a promising crafter's career at stake over this, but he realized that Dug was already moaning. It was an especially long and complicated moan. When it was finished, Dug turned to Bacca and smiled through his withered zombie lips.

"mmmm*Very* well," said the zombie king. "Then it is agreed. We have a bargain."

"Dug, what did you just do?" Bacca asked.

"mmmm*I* said yes," Dug replied.

"No, Dug, this is too much. It's not guaranteed that we will succeed. No crafter is perfect, even the best ones."

"mmmm*It's* what I want to do," Dug said. "Besides. We will succeed. I know it."

"mmmm*There* you have it," said the Zombie King. "The pact is made. I will order my generals to stand down for exactly seven days, and no more. If there is anything else we may do to help you in your mission, you have only to ask."

Bacca realized that much more was at stake than just some trampled crafter creations. The outcome of this quest could determine the future of all zombie crafters in the Overworld.

"There is *one* more thing," Bacca said. "Before we leave, I would like to see the room with the gold and emerald blocks where the skeletons stole the Bonesword. There may be clues inside that will help me."

"mmmm*Yes*," said the Zombie King. "Drooler will be happy to show you."

The zombie in the diamond armor looked surprised, then annoyed. He took a few shambling steps toward Bacca and Dug.

"mmmm*It's* this way," he said reluctantly. "C'mon. Follow me."

Drooler led Bacca and Dug out of the throne room and through a series of winding passageways. Apparently, word of their visit had gotten around Gravehome. The zombies they passed in the hallways now pointed and made long, complicated moans as Bacca and Dug passed. Bacca felt like even more of a celebrity than usual.

After traversing a long corridor of sandstone stairs, they arrived at a door framed with bright blue lapis lazuli blocks. This was the ceremonial room where the Bonesword was kept.

Drooler opened the door and the trio made their way inside. It looked much as Drooler had described it. Two zombie sentries were standing guard on either side of the granite platform flanked by blocks of gold and emerald. Bacca thought it was strange that the guards were still there, since the Bonesword was long gone.

Bacca examined the room carefully. The stone slabs and blocks of stone bricks that composed the walls looked strong and impenetrable. He ran his paws carefully across the walls. There did not seem to be any secret passages or trap doors. There were pressure plates on the floor, but the skeletons might have avoided these. There was only one entrance to the room—and that was the way they'd come in.

Looking up, Bacca saw that the ceiling stretched high into the darkness above.

"You say they escaped up there?" Bacca asked, gesturing up toward the blackness with his paw.

"mmmm*Exactly*," Drooler said. "After they tied me up. They climbed ropes up to the ductwork in the ceiling. Then they pulled the ropes up after them. It was cleverly done, like they'd been planning it a long time."

"Are these the guards that were on duty that night?" Bacca asked.

"mmmm*No*," Drooler said. "I fired those two for abandoning their posts. They said they heard noises down the hallway and left to investigate, but they shouldn't have done that. Maybe the skeletons somehow made those noises to distract them."

Bacca nodded. Secretly, he wondered how skeletons had made noises *outside* of the room. It sounded fishy.

"How does it look to you?" Bacca whispered to Dug. "Any ideas? Anything you want to ask? Now's the time."

"mmmm*One* question," Dug began, speaking to Drooler in the common tongue for Bacca's benefit. "When they took the Bonesword and carried it up the rope with them, how did they hold it and climb the ropes at the same time?"

Much of Drooler's face had long since rotted away, but he still found a way to knit his forehead menacingly at this question.

"mmmm*What* do you mean how did they hold it?" Drooler said sternly.

"Yes, it *would* be tricky to hold a heavy bone sword and climb up a rope at the same time," Bacca said. "Especially if you only had thin little skeleton fingers. But I suppose they could have brought along some kind of skeleton backpacks in order to—"

"mmmm*Yes!*" Drooler all but screamed. "Backpacks. I forgot to mention that. They had backpacks. That's how they did it."

"I see," Bacca said, giving Dug a wink. "Clearly, we've taken up enough of your time, Mr. Drooler. Thank you for your help."

"mmmm*Oh* . . . all right then," said Drooler, suddenly brightening. "In that case, I will show you out."

"Very good," said Bacca.

Together, they followed Drooler out of the ceremonial chamber room and back down the passageway toward the exit to Gravehome. As they walked behind him, Bacca and Dug exchanged a glance.

Mob members were generally not good liars, and zombies might have been the very worst at it. One thing was clear to Bacca and Dug: whatever had *actually* happened to the Bonesword, Drooler was not telling them the truth.

CHAPTER FOUR

"What I don't get is *why* he's lying," Bacca said as Gravehome began to fade into the distance behind them.

They were headed for the jungle biome where the Skeleton King could be found.

Dug nodded thoughtfully, but had no answer.

"And you saw that ceremonial chamber," Bacca continued. "The ceiling was hundreds of feet high. If skeletons rappelled down that wall and back up again, I'll eat my . . . my . . . um. I was going to say 'eat my hat' but I don't wear a hat. Anyhow, I'll eat something very unpleasant. Like *cooked* fish."

Dug, who only ate raw human flesh (like any good zombie) agreed that this sounded most unpleasant.

"I don't even know if skeletons *can* climb ropes," Bacca continued. "I've never seen one do it. Nope, Drooler is definitely up to something."

"mmmm*What* do you think really happened?" Dug asked.

"I think Drooler—or somebody working for him—took the sword," Bacca replied. "Maybe to sell it. Maybe for some other reason that I can't think of. But that's definitely what happened."

"mmmm*Or* maybe Drooler works for the skeletons," Dug theorized.

"Hey, that's not a bad idea," Bacca said. "The skeletons could have paid him, or made him some other kind of promise. But that still doesn't answer why the skeletons want the Bonesword in the first place."

"mmmm*So* . . . what are we going to do at the skeleton temple?" Dug asked.

"Exactly what we said we'd do," Bacca answered. "We've heard from the zombies. So let's see what the skeletons have to say for themselves."

Bacca was a free-spirit and didn't like to be serious, but it suddenly occurred to him that he ought to bring up something serious with Dug.

"Before we go any further, I want to talk to you about something," Bacca said. "That wasn't cool of the Zombie King to put you on the spot like that. Nobody should have to risk their status as a crafter in order to complete a quest, even an important one. I can't ask you to do that. And he certainly can't."

"mmmm*I* am confident that we will succeed," the zombie said. "Besides, nobody made me agree to that bargain. I wanted to do it."

Bacca thought that Dug was being very brave. Or very foolish. He wasn't entirely sure which.

"Okay, but it still doesn't seem right to me," said Bacca sheepishly.

Aware that they were now on the clock—the Zombie King had only given them one week to complete their task—Bacca and Dug journeyed as quickly as they could across the Overworld. They passed through many different biomes, until finally they began to see signs of the jungle where the skeletons dwelled. The sky was full of tall, healthy jungle trees. There were ferns and jungle flowers all across the landscape, and mysterious swaying vines dangling down from the canopy above. The land was also filled with ominous-looking temples made from giant blocks of moss stone and covered with leaves.

Dug realized that Bacca was headed toward the largest and mossiest of them all. He had never seen it firsthand, but Dug knew that the Skeleton King lived in a jungle temple that was far bigger than all the rest. The thought of being around so many skeletons—especially when the zombies were at war with them—made Dug nervous. So far, they hadn't actually seen any skeletons, but Dug thought he could hear their bones clicking in the distance . . . although it might have only been the sound of the jungle branches creaking in the wind.

"mmmm*Never* been here before," Dug said, looking around nervously.

"Neither have I," Bacca said.

This did not exactly inspire Dug with confidence.

"But don't worry," Bacca added. "Word about me has gotten around. I've dealt with skeletons before. And by 'dealt with' I mean 'smashed with my dia-mond axe.' Let's just say that most skeletons that see me coming these days turn around and start heading the other way."

No sooner were these words out of Bacca's mouth, than Dug did see some skeletons. They were standing along the walls of one of the temples in the distance.

"Steady now," Bacca said.

As Bacca and Dug drew closer, the skeletons walked around and clucked their bony clucks to one another, but they did not attack.

"mmmm*Did* you say earlier that you'd never met the Skeleton King?" Dug asked as they neared the immense, vine-draped temple that was their destination.

"That's right," replied Bacca. "But I know *of* him. The skeletons have a king just like you zombies do. What makes me curious is this idea that zombies and skeletons don't like one another. The Zombie King seemed really confident that skeletons are jealous of zombies, but I've never heard that. Never seen it either. Mob members will sometimes fight with other mobs, but it's not *personal,* you know?"

"mmmm*Yes,*" Dug said. "I have tangled with some witches a time or two, for example, when they got aggressive and annoying. Like coming over and bragging too much about how they were good at brewing potions. It's like, okay, I get it. You can brew potions. Why do you need to tell me about it? Who exactly are you trying to convince, ladies? You come off as a little insecure, if you ask me."

"But you don't have anything against witches *as a group* right?" Bacca said.

"mmmm*Not* at all," Dug replied. "Eventually they always realize I'm not interested in their potions and they go away and it's over."

"See, exactly," Bacca said. "That's how it works with most mobs. But the zombies in Gravehome seem to think that the skeletons have something against you guys on a deeper level."

"mmmm*That* would be news to me," Dug said.

"Yeah, me too," replied Bacca.

They reached the foot of the temple. It was located at the very center of the jungle biome where the trees were so thick overhead that it seemed to be always night. Because of this, the skeletons could move outside at any time of day. A long staircase of cobblestone stairs led up to a bigplatform in front of the temple entrance. The giant blocks were thick with moss. A few skeletons could be seen along the ramparts, but loud clicking sounds hinted at many other skeletons lurking nearby. Dug knew that this had to be the temple of the Skeleton King.

Bacca and Dug began the long, slow trek up the staircase. By the time they reached the top, the Skeleton King was there waiting for them. Dug could tell that he was the king because he was wearing a crown made from human finger bones, and he had the largest bow Dug had ever seen. A long white beard was attached to his chin bone. Skeleton soldiers stood to either side of him. (For the moment, their bows were not raised.) At one end of the temple platform, a pair of spider jockeys—seated astride huge, snarling spiders—gripped their reins hard to keep their bucking mounts at bay.

It was even harder to tell a skeleton's facial expression than a zombie's, but Bacca had the distinct impression that the king was sizing him up. The Skeleton King waited patiently as Bacca and Dug edged closer. He spoke in a voice filled with tiny, bony clicks.

"Who are you, and why have you brought a zombie here?" the king clicked.

He was direct, if nothing else. Bacca appreciated that.

"I'm Bacca," said Bacca. "I think you might have heard of me."

Some of the zombies clicked excitedly to one another.

"Yes, we have heard of you," said the king. "You are a great crafter. And a great warrior, too. But none of that explains why you are here at our temple with a *zombie*. Do you not know that a state of war exists between his kind and mine?"

"Good news on that, actually," Bacca said brightly. "I just negotiated a cease-fire with the Zombie King."

The Skeleton King opened his bony mouth, but no sound came out. He was aghast. (Which was not quite as bad as being an *actual* ghast, but still quite startling.)

"Thank you . . ." Bacca said sarcastically, ". . . is something you might say in return. Anyhow, it'll last a week. Longer if you agree to give back the Bonesword."

"What!?" the Zombie King cried. "The Bonesword? Is *that* what this is all about? They think we took their stupid relic?"

"Well . . . did you?" Bacca asked.

"Of course not," cried the king. "Why would we? We don't even use swords. Every skeleton knows that bows are the only true weapon."

The skeleton soldiers next to the king raised up their bows to show that this was true.

"I'll stick with axes myself, but to each his own," Bacca said, while thinking that the skeletons did have a point. How many had he ever seen with a sword? He struggled to come up with a single one.

"Why in the Overworld do the zombies think we took the Bonesword?" the Skeleton King pressed.

"Funny you should ask that," Bacca replied. "One of the top zombies named Drooler swears he actually *saw* your people take it."

"If I find out that any of my skeletons so much as—" the king began.

Bacca didn't let him finish.

"Relax," Bacca said. "I know that skeletons *didn't* take it. But the only way I could get the zombies to agree to a truce was to say I'd get it back from you."

The Skeleton King's bony body language told Bacca that he found this plan irritating.

"Then what are we going to do?" asked the Skeleton King. "Did you even think about that?"

"We have a week to figure out a plan," said Bacca. "A little less, actually. It was a long journey to get here."

"Perhaps you and I should take a walk and discuss this," the king said to Bacca. "Just you and I. What do you say? Once around the temple? I assure you, the tree canopy will keep me quite safe from the sun's effects."

"Okay," said Bacca. "Will my friend Dug be all right with your soldiers? They look pretty menacing, and he's just a kid."

"No harm will come to him," said the king. "If my friends seem a bit . . . *aggressive,* it is only because so many of our kind have perished at the hands of zombies in the past few days."

Bacca turned to Dug.

"Are you okay to hang out here?" Bacca asked.

"mmmm *Yes,*" Dug said brightly. "I have always wanted to see a spider jockey up close."

"Well, now's your chance," said Bacca.

As Dug made his first-ever attempt to pet a spider jockey's spider, Bacca followed the Skeleton King down the long stone staircase at the front of the temple to the jungle floor below, and the two began to walk in a circle around the great temple. Skeleton guards stationed along the tops of the temple walls looked down at them from far above.

Bacca realized that the king was never truly out of sight from his soldiers. And these looked to be the best soldiers of all. The slightly unnerving thought that he was always in range of one of their powerful bows never left Bacca's head.

"I thought we should discuss this away from your friend," the Skeleton King began. "I wouldn't want to offend him."

Bacca wondered what the king could possibly have to say that he didn't want Dug to hear.

"Tell me, how much do you know about zombie leadership?" the Skeleton King asked.

"Uh, they have a ruler, just like skeletons do," Bacca said. "A king or a queen."

"When do you choose a new king or queen?" pressed the Skeleton King. "And before you answer, 'When the old one dies,'" remember that skeletons and zombies do not suffer from old age in quite the same way crafters do."

Bacca was stumped.

"I guess I don't know," Bacca said. "Do *you* know?"

"I'm afraid I do," said the Skeleton King. "With the zombies, their king or queen stays in power only while their kingdom is prosperous. If there is a problem—if their fortress collapses, say, or they lose a war, or they run out of yummy crafters to eat—they believe that the Overworld is telling them that it's time for a new king or queen. So they pick a new one."

"And what happens to the old one?" Bacca inquired.

The Skeleton King stopped walking.

"The Bonesword happens," said the Skeleton King. "I thought that was obvious."

"Yikes," said Bacca, feeling ever gladder than usual that he wasn't a zombie.

"And losing the Bonesword has the same penalty," the Skeleton King continued, resuming his gait. "They just don't use the Bonesword to carry it out."

"No wonder the Zombie King wants the sword back so bad," Bacca said. "I'd be the same way if my neck was on the line!"

"He is in a very hard position," agreed the Skeleton King. "If he admits he has no idea where the Boneword is, then he's saying he's lost it. And you know what happens then. So he has to say that *we* have it, and he's just retrieving it from a temporary hiatus."

"Now this situation is becoming a little clearer," Bacca said.

"You can say that again," replied the Skeleton King. "We were wondering why these armies of zombies were attacking us so aggressively."

An idea occurred to Bacca.

"One more question," Bacca said. "Supposing the zombies *do* get rid of their current ruler. How do they choose the next one?"

"Oh, it usually goes to another high ranking zombie," the Skeleton King explained. "Like a general or a diplomat or . . ."

"The king's top advisor?" interjected Bacca.

"Yes, exactly," said the Skeleton King. "Whichever one is closest to the throne."

A piece of the puzzle fell into place in Bacca's mind.

"In that case," said Bacca. "I think I know what Dug and I need to do next."

CHAPTER FIVE

I t was a very dark time of night. The darkest, in fact. That which comes directly before dawn.

All in all, a bad time of night for a zombie to be out and about.

Which was exactly Drooler's problem.

The moment the sun's rays crept over the horizon, he would—like all adult zombies—start burning. It was a prospect he very much did not look forward to. Still, he tried to steel his resolve and be brave. He reminded himself, this was an important task, and a risk worth taking.

So that no one recognize him, Drooler had removed his distinctive diamond armor. Now he wore only rags, and while it was indeed very unlikely that anyone would ever believe that the king's top advisor would be dressed in such lowly attire, the costume made him even more vulnerable to the sun.

Drooler looked nervously up at the horizon. Was it his imagination, or were there already traces of pale blue in the sky?

The disguised zombie was standing near an arch of stone bricks and polished andesite along the outer perimeter of Gravehome. Snow was gently falling and the wind whipped his rags around. It was very cold. It was also quiet and empty. This was a remote part of the fortress exterior where almost nobody ever went. That was intentional. Drooler had selected the spot exactly for this quality.

Where were *those witches?!* he thought to himself.

In an ironic twist, the very same moment that this question crossed Drooler's mind, he saw movement in the shadows nearby.

Three mysterious figures stepped out into the dim moonlight. They wore purple robes with green stripes down the middle. They had long, bulbous noses. On each of their heads was a tall black hat, pointy like a cone, and with a big brass buckle on the front.

The wind shifted, and even Drooler—who, being a zombie, did not have a great sense of smell—couldn't help but catch of a whiff of chemicals. It was the scent of the powerful potions that witches were always brewing. It stuck to their clothes. You could smell it on them wherever they went. Drooler didn't want to be impolite. He fought the urge to hold his nose. (Drooler's nose had actually rotted off years ago, and was now removable. But he didn't want to hold it in his pocket. He wanted to pinch it shut to fight off the horrible smell.) Drooler reminded himself that witches could be dangerous. Each one of them probably carried several powerful Potions of Harming in her inventory, along with other dangerous things that Drooler didn't know about. Or *want* to know about. Offending a witch could be dangerous. A good way to do that, Drooler reasoned, was to let them know you thought they smelled like a chemistry set gone bad.

The witches did *not* look happy to see Drooler. Despite this, he tried to contort his zombie lips into something approaching a smile. He fought off the urge to gag.

"mmmm*Good* evening, ladies," Drooler said in his most pleasant tone of voice. "How lovely to see you again! You're certainly looking well. It's remarkable the way you're all able to keep those exquisite hats on your heads in this wind."

"Can it!" barked one of the witches. "This is no time for small talk. What do you want?"

"Yeah," barked another witch. "Why did you need to see us again? We've got busy schedules. Potions to brew. Crafters to annoy."

"And why are you wearing those ridiculous rags?" said the final witch. "You look like a pile of clothes somebody left outside in the rain."

To Drooler, the witches appeared almost completely identical. He had given up on telling them apart individually. Because of this, he was always careful to address them as a group.

"mmmm*Yes*, ladies," Drooler said. "Of course, I wouldn't want to waste your valuable time. I called you here regarding a very important matter."

"Out with it!" hissed one of the witches. Drooler could not tell which one had spoken.

"mmmm*Well* . . . erm . . . you know that thing that I asked you to do for me?" Drooler began, suddenly sounding less sure of himself.

"Of course we remember," said one of the witches. "Don't be stupid! That's the whole reason you came and found us. It's not like we're neighbors who bumped into each other at the store!"

Drooler had gone out of his way to arrange a partnership with the witches in the days leading up to his crime. He had heard they were good at keeping secrets, and also that nobody messed with them (namely, because they were quick to throw potions at anybody who did). And while both of these components of their reputation had proved accurate, Drooler had realized too late that witches were also very grumpy and hard to work with . . . which actually made a lot of sense, the more he thought about it.

"You're not trying to change our bargain are you?" one of the witches said accusingly. Her hand hovered near her inventory. Drooler knew that the wrong response would mean a vial of something nasty thrown in his face and several hearts of damage. Witches were said to draw their potions with startling swiftness, a claim supported by the fact that a witch had taken home the gold medal for Quick Draw in every Overworld Olympics dating back as far as anyone could remember.

"mmmm*No*, of course not," Drooler said. "You will still get all the diamond blocks in the zombie treasury . . . just as soon as they make me the new king."

"And all the fermented spider eyes in your laboratories," added one of the witches. "So we can make more potions. Don't forget about them."

"mmmm*Yes*, absolutely," Drooler said. "You will get those too."

"Well . . . okay then," said the witches, more or less in unison. "In that case, what do you want?"

"mmmm*You* know how I asked you to hang onto the Bonesword for a while—to keep it safe for me?" Drooler began carefully. "What if, instead, I needed you to get rid of it? Like, forever?"

The witches did not immediately respond. They looked at one another, then looked back at Drooler.

The zombie could almost hear the dangerous potions steaming and burbling in their inventories, waiting to splash all over him. He squinted his eyes, and prepared for some splashy-burny pain.

"mmmm*It's* just that this has gotten much more complicated than I ever thought it would," Drooler cried, hoping the witches would not fire.

Drooler was telling the truth. Initially, his evil plan had seemed so simple. How could it *not* work? He would steal the Bonesword from the ceremonial chamber, and give it to the witches for safe keeping. Then he would blame the theft on skeletons. In accordance with tradition, the Zombie King would be removed from office. And the next most important zombie (Drooler!) would be made the new king. After that happened . . .

Well, like most criminals, Drooler had not thought much past the part of the plan where he got what he wanted. He assumed that he would eventually be able to "find" the Bonesword somewhere in the Overworld—possibly by pretending to get it back from the skeletons, possibly by pretending to win a glorious battle against them (Yay, Drooler!)—and then return it to its rightful place. The other zombies would doubtless take this "victory" as another sign that Drooler had always been meant to rule them.

And, at first, it had looked like he was going to pull it off. He took the Bonesword out of the ceremonial chamber without a hitch, and he got his friendly (well, at least it started out that way) local witches to take it off his hands until the heat died down. So far, so good. But then it started to spiral out of control. Instead of making him the new king, the other zombies hesitated. There was no call for the current Zombie King to step down. Many top zombies argued that the Bonesword was not truly "lost" if they knew who had it. And because of Drooler's lies, they did. Or thought they did. Then things *really* got out of hand! The zombies' armies were called up and marched out to fight the skeletons. Everyone suddenly felt very proud to be a zombie, pulling together to fight for their zombie history, and the current Zombie King became more popular than ever. Drooler was further from the throne than before!

As if all of that weren't bad enough, the nearby crafters had gone and complained to Bacca. Now *he* was on the case! (Despite the failure of this latest plot, Drooler was actually quite clever and worldly. You didn't get to be the Zombie King's right hand man without keeping an ear to the ground. Not only had Drooler heard of Bacca, he'd heard enough to know that Bacca was the kind of crafter who could solve very tricky mysteries. Like, the mystery of who stole the Bonesword.) Now Drooler was nervous. Very nervous. It was only a matter of time until Bacca figured out what was really going on.

So Drooler decided it was time to do something drastic. It was time to get rid of the evidence. Even if that meant . . .

"mmmm*I* want you to get rid of the Bonesword," Drooler repeated his request to the witches.

Each one of the high-hatted ladies flashed the same evil, Cheshire grin.

"Where?" asked one of the witches. "We can't just throw it in the trash."

"mmmm*I* don't know," said Drooler. "In fact, I think it's better if I don't know."

The witches began to whisper confidentially. Every few moments, one of them cast a look in Drooler's direction. The zombie waited hopefully. Before long, they seemed to have reached an agreement.

"We will be able to perform the service you request," one of them eventually said.

This was a great load off Drooler's mind. He exhaled deeply, for dramatic effect. But, because—being a zombie—he did not actually *need* to breathe, Drooler was actually quite out of shape to perform a task many people did every day without even thinking about. So some cobwebs and a large hairball came up from his lungs. It was not very pleasant (for Drooler or for the witches).

"But there will be an additional charge," the witch continued.

"mmmm*Of* course," Drooler said anxiously. "Whatever you want. It, er, might take me a little longer than I originally planned to become the next zombie king. But don't worry. As soon as I do, you ladies can have anything you like from the treasury."

"This is not just about your treasury," one of the witches said. "If we dispose of the Bonesword, then you will have to do an *extra* favor for us."

"mmmm*A* favor?" Drooler asked. "What kind of favor?"

Then the witches began to tell the zombie exactly what they wanted him to do. As they spoke, their grins grew more and more wicked. Their teeth seem to glisten evilly in the moonlight, like long, sharp knives. It gave Drooler the creeps, big time.

"mmmm*That*?" the zombie said when they had finished. "But . . . but why do you want me to do *that*?"

In the distance, they heard a rooster crow. Looking up, Drooler saw that the sky had begun to lighten.

"There is no time to bicker," said one of the witches. "Do we have a deal? Yes or no?"

Drooler was filled with anxiety. Still, he had come this far. If one more deal was what it took to fix this mess, then he would do it. There was no turning back.

Drooler gave another superfluous sigh and nodded to the witches. They began to cackle loudly in excitement.

The zombie turned and hurried back along the perimeter of Gravehome, hoping to return to his room within the fortress before he was missed. As he hustled through the last moments of night, the cackling echoed in his ears. He wondered what he'd gotten himself into. Worry filled the pit of his stomach. And seeing as how Drooler had several actual pits in his stomach (along with holes, quite a few rocks, and at least one baby cave spider), this arrangement could only be more bad news for the zombie.

CHAPTER SIX

"**M**mmm *They* were friendly. For skeletons." Dug looked up at Bacca, wondering if his teacher would agree.

"I guess so," Bacca said. "But keep in mind, they had a *reason* to be nice. They want this war over as badly as we do. Once this is all cleared up, they're going to go back to taking potshots at everybody and everything."

Bacca and Dug were headed away from the skeleton temple, and had already reached the edge of the jungle biome. The trees were not so tall here, and vines no longer hung down from above. The dawn was just starting to break. Up ahead of them, a battalion of perhaps five hundred skeletons hurried in the opposite direction, hoping to make it back before the sun crested over the horizon. As they passed, Bacca stopped one of the skeleton soldiers.

"Fought any zombies today?" Bacca asked a skeleton. He looked like he might be high-ranking. The bones on his chest were polished to a gleam, like medals.

"Funny enough, no," the skeleton answered with many bony clicks. "Your friend here is the first one we've seen all day, and he looks a little young to be on the battlefield. It's almost like the zombies have stopped fighting."

Pleased to see that the zombies were actually obeying the cease-fire, Bacca let the skeleton get back to his troops.

Bacca and Dug continued on their way. As the morning wore on, they passed through several different biomes. There were fields full of lush flowers that waved in the breeze, deserts with only cacti and dead bushes, and plateaus that were perfectly flat, where you could see a very long way in every direction.

"mmmm*Where* are we going?" Dug asked as they neared a forest biome. "When you came back from talking with the Skeleton King, you seemed to know just what to do."

"I have a hunch where to find our next clue," Bacca told his young apprentice. "That zombie Drooler is behind this, I'm sure of it. Didn't it sound a little suspicious that he was the only eyewitness? And that the two guards who usually watch the Bonesword just happened to be out of the room?"

"mmmm*Yes*, the guards," Dug said. "I forgot about them. Drooler said he fired them as punishment for losing the Bonesword."

"That's pretty convenient, if you ask me," Bacca said.

"mmmm*Do* you know where they are?" Dug asked.

"I have a hunch," Bacca said. "A *strong* hunch. Have your zombie parents ever talked to you about Rotpit?"

Dug cocked his head to the side, trying to think. (It was a very unnatural angle, nearly ninety degrees, which Bacca found a bit disturbing. However, to a zombie it was apparently quite comfortable. But Bacca was glad when Dug finally moved it back to its usual position.)

"mmmm*My* father has spoken of Rotpit, now that you mention it," Dug said. "He says it is a good place. A place where he wants to retire some day. If there were a lottery for zombies, it's where they would go after they won."

"Exactly," said Bacca. "Rotpit is the deepest, darkest-roofed forest biome in the entire Overworld. Zombies never have to worry about the sun there. And it's surrounded by villages. Whenever they're in the mood, the zombies in Rotpit can venture out and have their pick of places to attack."

"mmmm*Wow!*" Dug said. "That sounds like heaven for a zombie. Why don't all zombies live there?"

"Well, for one it's not cheap," Bacca said. "Your own plot of ground there costs a whole lot of money. Rotpit real estate is outrageously expensive."

"mmmm*I* guess that makes sense," Dug replied.

"So, if I were a low-level guard from Gravehome who suddenly needed to disappear . . . and suddenly had more money than I knew what to do with . . ."

Dug nodded to say that he followed.

"Anyhow," Bacca said, "Rotpit is just up ahead. We'll find out shortly if my hunch is correct. But I'm pretty darn sure it is."

Bacca and Dug journeyed toward a dark forest biome on the horizon. Along the way, they passed several small villages. These villages showed signs of near-constant attack by zombies. The blocks of all the buildings were full of scratches caused by zombie fingernails. Most of the doors looked as though they had been destroyed and rebuilt at least ten times after zombies had bashed them down. Bacca decided the villagers who lived here must be especially hardy souls.

Past the ring of villages, they entered a dark roofed forest with enormous oak trees and a roof of leaves so dense that it completely blocked out the sun. The ground underfoot was lush and filled with many different kinds of mushrooms and rose bushes. There were also signs that this place saw heavy traffic from zombies. The soil was full of zombie footprints, and here and there were scattered pieces of zombie that had fallen off unbeknownst to their owners.

A few yards into the tree canopy, a zombie was standing guard. He wore a set of leather armor and held a rusty iron sword. He did not look happy to see visitors.

"Follow my lead, kid," Bacca whispered out of the corner of his mouth.

As Bacca and Dug neared the guard, the guard held up his weapon.

"mmmm*Halt*!" the zombie guard said. "I don't recognize either of you. This is a private, gated community for members only."

Bacca looked around.

"I don't see a gate anywhere," Bacca said.

"mmmm*We're* working on that," the zombie guard acknowledged. "Anyhow, you still can't come in."

"This is my friend Dug," Bacca said. "He's recently inherited a large sum of money. Take a look."

Here, Bacca opened his own inventory and allowed the zombie guard to take a look. It was full of diamonds, emeralds, and gold.

The guard smiled and lowered his sword.

"I'm Dug's assistant," Bacca continued. "I help manage his affairs. Now that Dug's a very rich zombie, he's interested in buying a plot here in Rotpit. Is there someone we could talk to about that?"

"mmmm*Of* course," said the guard. "Why didn't you say so in the first place? Right this way."

The zombie turned around and led Bacca and Dug down the path that led deeper into Rotpit. It was very dark and the earth underfoot was soft and moist—a perfect environment for the undead. Bacca and Dug began to pass groups of well-to-do zombies, out for a leisurely shamble. They looked very well-fed, and like they didn't have a care in the world. They were chatting about the new raids they had planned for that evening, and about an upcoming zombie masquerade ball. In all his years as a zombie, Dug had never heard of anything so decadent!

The zombie guard stopped in front of a small building made of polished granite blocks. Bacca thought it looked quite a bit like a grave marker. Perhaps that was the idea.

"mmmm*This* is the realtor's office," the guard said, knocking on the door. "I'm sure they'll be able to show you something nice."

After a few moments, another zombie emerged from the monument-like structure. She wore a large moth-eaten red blazer with holes worn in the elbows, and had stray clumps of long blonde hair clinging to her skull. She looked curiously at Bacca, but then smiled down at Dug. The zombie guard explained the situation.

"mmmm*Oh*, we will certainly be able to help you, young man," said the zombie real estate agent. "We've got lots of excellent spots available in some of the best neighborhoods in Rotpit. Just what an enterprising young zombie like yourself is looking for."

The zombie real estate agent led Bacca and Dug along the central path that ran through Rotpit's main district. There were plots of land available for sale, and many of them already had headstones made from fancy materials like polished granite, polished diorite, and polished andesite. Bacca was no expert, but it all looked very high-end, very posh.

"mmmm*Let* me know if you see anything you like," the agent said. "There are lots of options. We have everything from urban mausoleum condo conversions, to the more traditional midcentury headstone dwellings. And every neighborhood here is vibrant and diverse—by which I mean 'full of walking dead people.' The villagers in the area are also a treat. They practically *want* to get raided by zombies. It's a very good arrangement."

"Dug is still making up his mind," Bacca said. "We're not sure Rotpit is the perfect place for him. We're looking at some other locations too."

The zombie real estate agent was clearly annoyed by this, but did her best to keep smiling. Most of her lips had rotted away, so this was not particularly hard.

"I wonder . . ." Bacca continued. "Are there any new zombies who moved in recently? Maybe Dug could talk to them about what it's like here. That would sure help Dug make his decision."

"mmmm*Oh*, that's an excellent idea," the zombie real estate agent said enthusiastically. "And I know the perfect subjects. Two zombies from Gravehome just joined us a couple of weeks ago. We'll go find them right now. You can imagine how much they must like Rotpit if they left the zombie capital for it."

"mmmm*That* sounds good," Dug said, playing along.

The zombie real estate agent took Bacca and Dug to a freshly landscaped patch in central Rotpit. There were modern-looking headstones and monuments where trendy young zombies had made their homes. She indicated a couple of zombies milling around beside a large mausoleum made of redstone with obsidian accents. It looked very classy.

"mmmm*There* are the new zombies I was telling you about," said the real estate agent. "They opted for one of our premium models. Very popular with the younger set. Perhaps your friend—Hey, where are you going?!"

But Bacca was already charging over to the zombies at top speed.

"You two!" Bacca cried. "Yeah, you! I need to have a word."

Bacca could tell from their faces that they knew they had been caught.

"mmmm*Uh* oh," one of the zombies said.

"'Uh oh' is right," Bacca replied. "You two are in a heap of trouble. I've got some questions, and I expect some honest answers."

Bacca grinned just enough to show his fangs. He could be very intimidating when he wanted to.

The zombies hung their heads.

"I can guess how it happened, but I want to hear it from you," Bacca said. "You can start at the part where a senior zombie named Drooler shows up and asks if you'd like to make a whole lot of money for just a little work."

The guilty zombies explained that—true to Bacca's suspicions—they had been approached by Drooler and offered a large sum to conveniently "forget" to go to work on a certain day.

"mmmm*But* honest . . . " one of the zombie guards pleaded. "We never thought he was going to do something like this! Taking the Bonesword? Starting a war? It's awful!"

"mmmm*That's* right," said the other zombie guard. "We thought he was just maybe going to borrow the Bonesword for a little while. I thought for sure he would put it back when he was done."

Bacca rolled his eyes.

"That doesn't make what you did any more acceptable!" Bacca snapped. "Now I want you both to think . . . Where would Drooler have taken the Bonesword? Did he name a location where he was going to hide it? He wouldn't be stupid enough to keep it in his own quarters."

The zombie guards shook their heads. Neither of them looked like they were lying. They really didn't know. Then one of the zombies raised a moldy, dried-up finger.

"mmmm*I* wonder if . . ." the zombie began, then backtracked. "Naw, probably not. Never mind."

"What?" Bacca said. "Every detail can potentially be important."

"mmmm*It's* just . . . *I* don't know precisely what Drooler did with the Bonesword," the zombie began. "But I *did* hear he was friends with some witches."

"mmmm*Yeah*, I heard that too," said the other guard. "People said they'd see Drooler hanging out with a witch."

"A witch?" Bacca asked. "Interesting. Which witch?"

The zombies looked at him blankly for a second, their tiny zombie brains trying to unravel Bacca's question.

"mmmm*Witch* witch?" one of them tried. "Are you saying the same word twice? Like Drooler Drooler."

Bacca rolled his eyes and shook his head in disbelief. Evidently, the smartest zombies were not selected for guard duty.

"mmmm*Maybe* he was staring a new sentence—a new sentence about a witch—and you just didn't give him time to finish," the other zombie said. "You're always doing that."

"mmmm*No* I'm not!" the first zombie protested.

Bacca rolled his eyes again.

After much confusion, one of them eventually got it, and explained that there was a coven of three witches who lived near Gravehome.

"mmmm*Drooler* tried to keep it a secret that he was friends with them, but everybody knew about it," one of the zombies said. "Word got around."

"I believe that," Bacca said. "It seems like villains always think they're better at keeping secrets than they actually are. Where can I find these witches?"

"mmmm*Just* northwest of Gravehome," the zombie guard explained. "They live in a hut supported by long columns that look like chicken legs. Traditional witch architecture, apparently. You can't miss it."

"Thanks," Bacca said, his tone turning stern. "Now, as for *you two* . . ."

The zombies gave Bacca a terrified look.

"I want you to sell your homes you bought here—the nice real estate zombie in the blazer can help you with that—and then I want you to march straight back to Gravehome and tell the Zombie King what you did."

"mmmm*Are* you crazy?" said one of the zombie guards. "Do you have any idea what the king will do to us?"

"If you prefer," Bacca said in a mischievous tone of voice, "I could always tell *these* zombies here in Rotpit what you did. They've heard about the war, and they're furious at the skeletons. How furious do you think they'll be when they learn that zombie soldiers went off to war for no reason? At least with the Zombie King, you'll have the opportunity to beg for mercy. I might even mention to him that you were helpful in my investigation. But with these privileged, rich zombies used to doing whatever they want . . . well, I would say your chances are probably not as good."

"mmmm*Okay,* okay," the zombie guards said. "We'll do what you say. Just . . . please don't tell anybody around here what we did!"

Bacca stepped back over to the zombie real estate agent. She was having a long, moan-y conversation with Dug.

"I've got some bad news, but I've also got some good news," Bacca told her. "The bad news is none of these plots look quite right for Dug."

"mmmm*That's* a shame," said the zombie real estate agent. "Are you sure? Did you see those monuments made of lapis lazuli blocks? They're very cutting edge."

"Yes, yes, they're quite nice, but they're not what Dug had in mind," Bacca insisted. "I have good news, though. Our two friends from Gravehome have decided they want to move back to the capital."

"mmmm*What?*" said the real estate agent, astonished. "But . . . but . . ."

"You didn't let me finish," Bacca said with a smile. "They're looking to sell the places they bought at a *significant loss*. In fact, I think they'll accept any offer. You'll make a lot of money."

"mmmm*Oh*," said the agent. "Well that *is* good news."

Without further ado, Bacca thanked the zombie real estate agent for her help, and he and Dug made their way out of Rotpit.

"mmmm*That* was a pretty cool place," Dug said when they were back on the road. "Maybe I'll be able to live there someday for real. I liked all the pretty headstones. The use of andesite accents was very well done. Though I think I could have done better."

"I think you could *definitely* do better," Bacca told him. "You're a crafter with real skill, and you should be thinking bigger than headstones."

"mmmm*Remember*, for a zombie, that's like a house," Dug said.

"Oh yeah," Bacca told him. "I guess I see your point."

"mmmm*Anyway,* what should we do now?" Dug asked. "The guards confessed to helping Drooler, right? So if they go tell the Zombie King what really happened, then he'll know the truth and he can arrest Drooler and call off the war. Then we can all go home, right?"

Dug was a great crafter, but Bacca realized he was still getting the hang of diplomacy.

"Not quite," Bacca said with a knowing grin. "Think about it. Even if they go back and admit what they did, the Zombie King is still in a tough situation. The Bonesword is still missing. He's still the king that lost it, so he's still in hot water. You better believe that I want everybody involved in this scheme to get the justice that's coming to them— especially that lousy jerk Drooler—but we've got to get the Bonesword back first. That's the only thing that really solves everything. Do you follow me?"

Dug nodded to say that he did.

"Meanwhile, this ceasefire between the zombies and the skeletons is going by fast. We've only got about five days left, by my counting."

"mmmm*So* what are we going to do next?" asked Dug.

"We're going to go see some witches," Bacca said confidently, and they began the trek back north to the Ice Plains Spikes Biome.

CHAPTER SEVEN

Once again, Drooler was terrified.

He had followed the witches' directions perfectly: South to the river, then through the Forest Biome until it gave way to savanna. Then savanna became taiga. Then southeast until he saw the big altar made of red sandstone. And there it was. The altar. Drooler had never seen one so enormous. That was what made him uneasy. That, and the other part . . .

The witches had told Drooler to set the Dragon Egg on the altar at precisely midnight. This should have been exhilarating, Drooler thought. Under other circumstances, it would definitely have been exhilarating. Or at least very, very interesting. Dragon Eggs were the rarest item in all of Minecraft. There was only one per server plane. Getting one was about the hardest thing you could do.

Drooler reached into his inventory and took out the egg. It was black and purple and very heavy. It felt like the kind of thing that a dragon would miss. Like, a dragon might come after whoever had stolen it. So, with shaking, nervous hands, Drooler placed it on top of the altar. Then he waited. A cool breeze blew across the taiga. The ferns swayed gently in the breeze. There was no other movement.

Then it happened.

A great rustling came from the direction of the spruce trees on the far side of the altar. The ground began to shake under Drooler's feet. A few of the trees actually began to bend or to fall over, as if some immense beast was trampling them.

Drooler swallowed hard. (Being a zombie, with very little saliva, this was actually quite an accomplishment.)

The rustling got closer and closer, until from out of the spruce trees emerged the largest wolf Drooler had ever seen. It had a silky grey coat and glowing red eyes. It stood several times taller than Drooler.

"mmmm*Nice* doggie," Drooler said as the enormous wolf approached the altar. Its eyes seemed to burn as if they actually were made of fire. What was this thing? Why was it here? Had a dragon sent it? What had those tricky witches gotten him into now?

Drooler knew that taiga biomes were full of wolves. He'd seen them many times. Sometimes crafters tamed them and kept them as pets. In rare cases, they could be friendly, even to zombies. But he'd never heard of wolves this big. As the enormous beast got closer and closer, Drooler felt less and less comfortable with its presence.

The wolf stood on the opposite side of the rectangular altar and looked at Drooler. Then it looked down at the Dragon Egg. It sniffed the egg and touched it with a paw, as if checking to see that it was real. Then the wolf looked up at Drooler and smiled.

"If you do that again, I will bite your head off," the giant wolf said matter-of-factly.

"mmmm*Do* what?" Drooler asked after another terrified gulp.

"Refer to me as 'doggie,'" it said. "I am neither a doggie nor a wolf, though my connection to both is very strong. I am the Spirit of the Taiga. I am connected to all creatures in taiga biomes throughout the Overworld. I am very powerful and very strong."

"mmmm*Gosh*," said Drooler. "Sorry for calling you a doggie."

Drooler began to feel that he was even more deeply in over his head than he had been before. If that were even possible.

"mmmm*Some* witches gave me this Dragon Egg and said I should put it on the altar and wait for somebody to come," Drooler continued hastily. "They said that when whoever arrived—and I'm feeling more and more sure that they were talking about you—I should tell you that this was an offering from the witches near Gravehome, and to ask if . . . if . . . it was 'enough.' I have no idea what that means. They didn't tell me anything else."

The enormous wolf smiled again, as if this amused him greatly.

"Those witches never give up, do they?" the wolf said.

"mmmm*What?*" asked Drooler, still confused. "I have no idea what is happening."

"It is tradition that visitors may present a gift to the spirits of different biomes, and ask a favor in return," explained the wolf. "This has got to be my ninth or tenth gift from the witches. And I must say, it *is* an improvement on their previous offerings."

"mmmm*What* do they usually send?" Drooler asked.

The wolf smiled again. Its mouth was enormous. Probably, it could swallow Drooler in a single gulp.

"Many of their gifts have been, frankly, terrible," the wolf said. "Blocks of diamond. Blocks of gold. Once they gave me a statue *of me*, made entirely out of granite, bedrock, and quartz. A statue of myself! Can you imagine? What am I going to do with *that*? If I want to know what I look like, I can just see my reflection in a lake."

Drooler nodded. The wolf was right about that. Lakes were plenty reflective.

"No, no, no," the giant wolf continued. "The previous gifts were *entirely* unacceptable. They were so unacceptable, in fact, that I had to eat the people who brought them. That's why the witches don't come personally. They know that I tend to punish those who bring me lousy gifts. It took three of their workers to bring the statue of me, as I recall. And then I had to eat *all three* of them!"

Drooler's knees knocked in terror as the full extent of his predicament became clear. Because he was a zombie, and his flesh was mostly dried up, this produced an actual knocking sound when his kneebones connected. It was like somebody playing just one note on a xylophone, over and over again. This made the Spirit of the Taiga chuckle.

"But . . ." the wolf continued, stifling further laughter. "I think perhaps the witches have finally presented a gift that is worthy of one of my favors. Dragon Eggs are the rarest of the rare. They cannot be mined or made. To obtain one usually means tangling with the Ender Dragon. Yes, all in all, I think this is a suitable gift."

The Spirit of the Taiga picked up the Dragon Egg and turned it over again and again, like a child playing with a new toy. Drooler realized that he was perhaps *not* about to be eaten by a giant wolf. For the first time in many hours, he began to relax.

"mmmm*So*, erm, what happens next?" Drooler asked. He was thinking at that moment that he'd like to return to a shadier biome before the sun came up. "Should I go back and tell the witches the good news? I could ask them the favor they want you to do. They didn't tell me what it was."

"Oh, I already know what the witches want," the wolf said in a sinister voice, never taking his eyes off the egg. "They've already made that abundantly clear. I may need to check with them regarding a few details, but the request is straightforward enough. Tell me, would *you* like to know what it is?"

"mmmm*Okay*," said Drooler, hoping that it was something good.

Then the Spirit of the Taiga leaned forward across the altar and whispered into Drooler's rotting ear. The zombie's eyes went wide. He couldn't believe what he had heard. In his wildest dreams, he had never imagined the witches could want anything like *that!*

As Drooler started to think about the implications—and the awful consequences for *him*—he began to wonder if being eaten by a giant wolf might just be preferable to the future that awaited.

It sure looked like a place where witches would live.

It was square hut with walls made of dark wooden planks. There were no windows. A single chimney of grey stone bricks stuck out of the slanted roof. But the most striking feature had to be the legs. Technically, they were stilts. They extended down from the base of the house, lifting it high off the ground. Looking closely, Bacca saw that they were made from a mix of polished diorite, polished granite, redstone, and gold blocks. The combined effect of this color scheme was to make the stilts look a whole lot like chicken legs, right down to the equally chicken-y looking feet.

"mmmm*Do* you think it can walk?" Dug whispered.

"I guess we're going to find out," Bacca said.

The hut did not walk away as they approached, but there also didn't seem to be a good way to knock on the door. Bacca could jump high, but not that high. Even with a Potion of Leaping, Bacca guessed he would still be several feet short.

"Hey!" he called, looking up at the door and cupping his hands to his muzzle. "Are you witches home? Come out and talk to us!"

There was no response.

"mmmm*Maybe* they went to the store or something?" Dug offered.

"Maybe," Bacca said. "But maybe not."

Bacca took a few steps back from the hut, and reached into his inventory. He pulled out a bow enchanted with Infinity and Flame. Bacca nocked an arrow and took aim.

"mmmm*You're* going to burn their house down?!" Dug asked in alarm.

"Relax," Bacca said with a smile. "I'm just going to get their attention."

Bacca fired several flaming arrows in a cluster at the center of the witches' front door. Dug looked on, curious. He had never seen anybody do anything like this. When Bacca finished firing, Dug realized that the arrows were in the shape of a "B." Dug thought it was a clever touch.

"It's important to sign your work," Bacca explained.

"mmmm*I* see," said Dug with a grin.

"Hey witches," Bacca shouted, putting his bow away. "I know you probably don't want to talk to us, but you should come out anyway. You might want to have a look at your door."

There was no movement from inside, and the flames began to spread.

Dug opened his mouth to moan something, but Bacca silently put up his paw, as if to say: "Just give it a moment longer. Something's going to happen. Probably, something pretty cool."

He was right. Only a few moments later, a very large and very annoyed-looking witch opened the door.

"Ahh!" she cried. "What have you done? My beautiful door!"

She took a bucket of water out of her inventory and quickly doused the flames.

"Hello," Bacca said. "Now that I have your attention, my name is Bacca, and this is Dug. We need to talk to you about something very important."

"That's what you think," the witch said, and slammed the door again.

Bacca sighed and nocked another flaming arrow. He shot it at the door, but the door did not catch on fire. It was now too wet.

"I guess we're going to have to do this the hard way," Bacca said.

"mmmm*What's* the hard way?" Dug asked.

"I'll show you," Bacca told him. "You can help with it."

Bacca took out Betty. Dug copied Bacca, and took out his own axe. Unlike Bacca's diamond weapon, Dug's was stone and enchanted with Unbreaking.

"Does your axe have a name?" Bacca asked his zombie apprentice.

"mmmmNo," Dug said. "But if we're going to do what I *think* we're going to do, then I will name it Chicken-Chopper."

Dug pointed to the legs holding up the witches' hut.

"I like the name, but let's look for a solution that's *con*structive, not *de*structive," Bacca said. "That's an important part of being a good crafter."

Instead of turning Betty loose on the legs of the hut, Bacca went over to a clump of tall spruce trees nearby and started chopping. Dug joined in. Soon, they had had enough blocks of spruce to craft a whole pile of planks. And after crafting those planks, they used their axes to begin carefully breaking them down into wood sticks.

Bacca noticed again and again what a skilled crafter his young zombie friend was. The sticks that Dug created were perfectly straight and very strong—seemingly much stronger than normal spruce sticks should have been. They could have made fine fishing poles, rails, fences, or any number of valuable objects.

"How are you at making ladders?" Bacca asked his star pupil.

"mmmm*They* say I make the best around," Dug answered.

"Oh really?" Bacca said. "That's high praise. Show me. We need a ladder that stretches all the way up to the witches' front door."

Dug nodded and got to work. He stitched the spruce sticks together to form a long ladder with many rungs. Bacca watched him closely. Every stitch was true. Dug seemed to have done this many times before. He held up the finished product for Bacca to inspect. Bacca had never seen a finer ladder. It would probably hold ten or twenty iron golems at once.

"Not bad," Bacca said. (Inside, he was thinking: *Holy cow! This kid is good!*)

Bacca took the ladder and attached it to the right front chicken leg so that it reached all the way up to the witches' door.

"mmmm*They're* going to be mad we chopped down their spruce trees," Dug said as he and Bacca began their climb.

"I hope they're going to be very, *very* mad," Bacca said. "Because mad people—especially mad witches—tend to make mistakes."

"mmmm*Mistakes* like telling us where the Bonesword is?" Dug asked.

"Now you're catching on," Bacca said.

They climbed the ladder to the front of the hut until they were face-to-face with the front door.

Bacca raised a paw to knock on the door, then hesitated.

"Have you chatted with witches before?" he asked Dug. "Like, have you ever really gotten to know one?"

The zombie shook his head no.

"mmmm*My* only experience has been fighting with them."

"Witches are mean and self-centered," Bacca explained. "That comes across when they're throwing potions at you, but also in conversation. They're also quick to get angry, and even quicker to get paranoid and suspicious. That's what we're going to count on today. Remember, the objective here is not necessarily for us to win and for the witches to lose. The objective is to get the Bonesword back."

"mmmm*So* what do you recommend?" Dug asked.

"I'd put away the axe, for starters," Bacca replied.

Dug placed his axe back into his inventory.

"Good," said Bacca. "For the rest of it . . . just follow my lead. The good thing about covens is that it means there'll be several witches. We can also use that to our advantage. Watch and learn."

Dug didn't immediately understand how more witches was less of a problem, but he decided to take Bacca's word for it.

Bacca rapped hard on the witches' front door.

"Hello, witches!" he cried. "Any chance we could have a word with you? We're right here outside your door!"

Moments later, the door opened and a powerful Potion of Harming sailed through. Only lighting-quick reflexes saved Bacca from a nasty splash and several hearts of damage.

"What's the big idea?" Bacca asked in an annoyed voice. "I already told you, I just came by to talk. And it's about something *important*."

Silence followed. Bacca peered inside the doorway. Despite the impressive chicken-legs, the interior was very much like other witch huts. The ceiling was low, and the layout was a single square room. It was filled with various witch-y amenities, including burbling cauldrons for brewing potions and tables filled with exotic ingredients. Beside the door was an umbrella holder containing exotic looking broomsticks. Of course, the thing that really drew Bacca's eye was the witches. There were three of them in total. They were very large. Their tall, pointy hats stretched so high that they rubbed against the ceiling of the hut. They did not look happy to have visitors. All three had potions of harming cocked and ready to throw.

"Let's try this one more time," Bacca said. "My name is Bacca. Maybe you've heard of me?"

At least a couple of the witches had. He saw them flinch when he said his name.

"Good," Bacca said, taking a careful first step inside of the hut. "Glad to know my reputation precedes me. My awesome, *awesome* reputation."

"Why are you here, and what do you want?" growled a witch. "Speak quickly. We've no time for chatting."

"Yes, you're interrupting important witch business," said the second witch.

"Why shouldn't we just obliterate you with potions right now?" demanded the third.

"Well," answered Bacca, "then we wouldn't be able to work together anymo-"

Bacca put his paw to his mouth as though he had accidentally said something he shouldn't have. His eyebrows lifted, and he glanced back and forth quickly. He looked like someone who realizes he has just made a horrible mistake.

The effect upon the witches was instant. They glanced around the room nervously. It was clear that none of them knew quite how to proceed.

Witches were naturally distrustful of crafters (and zombies, for that matter), but that they were *especially* distrustful of other witches.

"What do you mean, 'work together'?" one of the three asked cautiously.

"Oh nothing," said Bacca. "I must have misspoke. I certainly didn't mean to imply that I have been working with one of the members of this coven. That we're practically old friends at this point. Or that I'm going to ask about the Bonesword. Oops! I did it again!"

Bacca put us paw up to his mouth in mock embarassment.

This time, the witches could not contain themselves. They physically moved away from each other, forgetting about Bacca and Dug almost entirely. They moved to different sides of the hut. Their hands still hovered over their potions, ready to draw, but now it looked as though they might target each other inside of their visitors.

"Who told him about the Bonesword?!" cackled one of the witches, turning to her colleagues. "Was it you? Was it *YOU*?"

"I didn't tell him!" said another witch. "It must have been *her*!"

"I didn't tell him either!" insisted the last witch. "But he couldn't have heard it from somebody else! Who else knows?"

The three witches glared at one another for a tense moment. Bacca did not want the witches to actually start throwing potions, if only because he needed them to tell him where they'd put the Bonesword. If they melted one another, he'd back to square one.

"Ladies, ladies," Bacca said, striding confidently to the center of the hut. "There's no need to argue about this. Forget I said anything. I don't know where I even got this crazy idea that I'm secretly friends with one of you."

Bacca winked at Dug, who watched in fascination from the doorway.

"The important thing," Bacca continued, "is that we trust each other going forward. And that you don't spend any more time worrying about which one of you told me all about holding onto the Bonesword for Drooler."

Dug would have said it was physically impossible for the witches to look any more alarmed. Dug would have been wrong.

The witches' faces screwed up into masks of mistrust, betrayal, and deep-seated anger. Their eyes narrowed to evil slits. Dug guessed the only reason they had not yet fired was they were choosing between two targets.

"He doesn't just know about the Bonesword!" howled a witch, cocking her potion. "He also knows about Drooler!"

"In that case," another witch said, "he probably also knows about the Fortress of Confusion."

One of Bacca's hairy eyebrows went up just a tic.

"That's right," Bacca said confidently. "The Fortress of Confusion. I know all about that too. It's the place where . . . um . . . where . . ."

Bacca snapped his fingers as if trying to recall something.

"Where we put the Bonesword when Drooler told us to get rid of it," said one of the witches.

"Oh, *that's* right," Bacca said.

"Well, technically, it's where we told the *bat* to put the Bonesword," another witch clarified. "Incidentally, I hope he makes it back okay. That fortress is dangerous, and he's my favorite pet. Though I'd never let him know."

"Yes, the bat!" said Bacca. "I knew all about him too. And this fortress . . . Which is located . . . ?"

The witches looked at Bacca.

"In the stone beach biome to the west, beside the ocean," said one of the witches. "But everybody knows that."

"Yes they do!" said Bacca. "Of course they do. In fact, anybody who said they didn't would probably be messing with you."

Bacca gave Dug another wink and nodded to the door. They had got what they came for. Now all that was left was to escape from this hut.

Bacca began to creep toward the door.

"Ladies, I think I've taken up enough of your valuable time. I can see that you're not in the mood to chat, so my friend and I had better be on our way. . . ."

Bacca slowly moved closer to the doorway where Dug lingered. He expected one of the witches to fire at any moment. Instead, something very unexpected happened.

One of the witches lowered her potion and said: "It occurs to me now that almost none of this will matter if Drooler is successful."

The other two witches thought about this for a second, then they too lowered their potions.

"Hey, you know what . . . you're right!" said a second witch. "Look at us, getting all hot and bothered about who told Bacca about the Bonesword. Pretty soon, the Bonesword will be *totally meaningless!*"

Bacca didn't like the sound of that.

"Yes!" said the final witch. "The clock is ticking. The zombies are about to have much bigger problems, aren't they? *Much* bigger problems!"

And the witches all began to cackle in unison. Cackling is like laughing, but it's when witches do it. And like almost everything witches do, it is much more disturbing than what you're expecting.

The cackling didn't stop as Bacca and Dug began to climb back down the ladder. Bacca thought it might even have gotten louder. It was hard to believe three people could make such a strange, scary sound.

"mmmm*Bacca*, what does that mean?" Dug asked as they climbed. "Why are they laughing like that?"

"Honestly, I don't know," Bacca replied. "But I think it means we need to get our hands on the Bonesword as quickly as possible."

CHAPTER EIGHT

The bat's name was Flappy.

When your name's Flappy, you're probably a bat. Or possibly a chicken. *Maybe* a ghast.

But bat is what you hope for. Bat is going to be at the top of that pecking order.

Flappy had been raised by the witches since he was a baby. Sometimes one of the witches even called him her "familiar." (This had always struck Flappy as odd, because the witches were actually quite distant and not really familiar with anybody.) Today, Flappy was running an errand for the witches. He ran errands for them all the time, but today's errand was special, they had told him. Flappy wasn't exactly sure what made it special, but he had to grant that it was more unusual and complicated than his ordinary work.

Most of the time, the tasks assigned to Flappy involved fetching things. The witches would send him out into the Overworld to gather ingredients, presumably for potions they were brewing. Flappy had become expert at finding trace amount of glowstone dust, tiny bits of redstone ore he could grip in his claws, and he even knew where the best melons grew for making glistering melons (which, in turn, he'd learned made Potions of Healing).

As Flappy flew higher and higher along the bleak landscape of stone cliffs, it occurred to him that he had never before been asked to *deliver* anything. His work started and ended with ingredient recovery. That was his wheelhouse. That was what he knew. But this was a new and strange request. This time he had to take something to a certain place in the stone beach biome and *drop it off.*

Very unusual.

Yet Flappy was not one to second-guess his trio of bosses. If they wanted something done, they probably had a good reason for it. (Like most people, Flappy had long since given up on trying to tell the witches apart. He now thought of them as purely interchangeable. It saved time, and freed up more energy to look for ingredients.)

Nearing his destination, Flappy looked down at the strange item the witches had placed in his claws. It didn't look like something that needed to be delivered to a whole other biome at the edge of the sea. No, not at all. It looked like something that needed to be thrown away. It was just an old bone. Sure, somebody—probably a crazy person, Flappy thought—had whittled it down so that one edge was very sharp. And then another person— probably even crazier—had carved all these intricate designs into it (designs that, now that Flappy looked closer, seemed to resemble zombies). But all the same. A bone was a bone was a bone, right? And why should anybody want to deliver a bone?

Flappy flew up a coastline of imposing cliffs and enormous waterfalls that sent rivers crashing down into the sea. Whenever Flappy saw another creature—whatever it was—he kept his distance. The witches had insisted that this delivery was "top secret" and "high priority." Flappy knew that when they used these words, it meant he should stay out of sight and not talk to anybody. Still, Flappy thought, how could an old bone be important enough that he needed to hide it? That was a mystery. Then again, when you were a bat, it was a mystery why anybody did anything other than snack on delicious insects under fruit trees all day. Mysteries, Flappy had decided, were better left to others.

Flappy rose high above the cliffs. The headwinds off the sea were very strong, and it was difficult to maintain airspeed. The bone—which was almost as big as Flappy himself—grew heavy in his grasp. The longer he flew, the worse this would get. If he wasn't careful, he might eventually drop it. Maybe into the sea. If this happened, the witches would be very upset indeed.

It was as this alarming thought began to percolate in Flappy's brain that he finally saw what he was looking for. On the horizon was a high, prominent cliff. It was different from the others around it. It jutted out like a crooked tooth sticking out of someone's mouth. As he got closer, Flappy saw that a crafter had carved something into the face of the cliff. As the bat drew nearer still, making swoops in the air to get a better view, he saw that it was a face. More precisely, a skull.

Just like the witches had said.

Flappy carefully made his way to the top of the cliff, preparing to land. As he flew closer, Flappy began to feel uneasy. Something about this place did not sit well with him—above and beyond the fact that it contained no tasty insects to munch on. Something about the skull carving was spooky. Scary. As if the empty eye sockets were looking right at him, watching him as he flew. It would be best to get this delivery over with as soon as possible, Flappy thought.

The tiny bat reached the top of the skull. He looked down and saw that the roof of the cliff—where the witches had said to leave the bone—was not solid. Instead, it was a crisscrossing pattern of iron bars. Flappy wondered if the witches intended that he should drop the bone through one of the holes between the bars.

Puzzled, and slightly frustrated that he wasn't given more specific instructions, Flappy swooped down to look for a place to land and think it over.

Before he knew what was happening, a long skeletal hand reached out from between the iron bars below. The fingers were wiggling and moving, as though the skeleton was alive. With a single swift movement, the hand snatched the bone right out from between Flappy's claws. Its grip was so strong! Flappy couldn't have held on if he'd wanted to. In a flash, the bone was gone, and the skeletal hand along with it.

Flappy had seen enough. Unburdened of his load, he soared high above the cliff, pointed himself in the opposite direction, and headed for home. He did not relax until the strange skeletal face was far in the distance.

Even though he had survived this encounter, Flappy decided that his delivery days were over. Familiar or not, Flappy resolved to tell the witches that, from now on, he was going to stick to gathering ingredients.

CHAPTER NINE

"**M**mmm*Fortress* of Confusion?"

It was a question.

"I've never heard of it,," said Bacca. "And I've heard of most things. Heck, I've *done* most things. I'm Bacca, after all. But this one is a mystery. I guess there *might* be a handful of places on this server plane that I don't know about. This 'Fortress of Confusion' must be one of them. Hmph. I wonder what's so confusing about it."

"mmmm*Maybe* it's confusing because you find yourself wondering why you haven't heard of it yet?" Dug said.

Bacca liked this roundabout logic. He and Dug had left the witches' hut behind some hours ago, and were now making their way across the Overworld in the direction of this strange new fortress.

"mmmm*I* have to say, I didn't enjoy hearing the way those witches were laughing," Dug added.

"Neither did I," Bacca replied. "It really creeped me out. It's like they know something we don't. Something bad."

"mmmm*Are* we heading straight for the stone beach biome—the place where the witches said this fortress would be?"

"Sort of," said Bacca. "We're going to make one stop along the way. I want to talk to the Skeleton King again. The jungle biome where the skeletons live is very close."

"mmmm*Why* him?" asked Dug.

"The point of all of this is to keep the zombies and skeletons from destroying everything under the sun—including each other," said Bacca. "We don't have much time left in the ceasefire. I don't know how long it will take us to get the Bonesword once we're inside this fortress, if we even succeed at all. So I'm hoping to convince Skeleton King to keep his soldiers home just a little longer."

"mmmm*And* the Zombie King?" asked Dug.

"The Zombie King is in a harder spot," replied Bacca. "If those guards actually go back and confess what they did—like I *told* them to—I think it might create enough uncertainty to make the Zombie King hesitate before he launches another offensive. That's what I hope happens, anyway."

"mmmm*This* is a very hard and confusing time," Dug said as they journeyed on. "Our mission—these things we are doing—they will have a great impact on many other people's lives. Knowing this creates a sensation which is new to me. It is not altogether pleasant. It makes me feel like there is something heavy on top of both my shoulders. Blocks of iron, perhaps."

"That's called 'responsibility,'" said Bacca. "And I'd be more worried if you *weren't* feeling it."

"mmmm*I* don't know if I like all this 'responsibility,'" replied Dug.

"Welcome to my world," Bacca said with a smile.

They journeyed west for several hours more, until they once again found themselves in skeleton territory. Squads of skeleton soldiers were milling about along the roads, waiting for word that the war was back on.

Past these soldiers, Bacca and Dug reached the great, central skeleton temple. They climbed the long staircase leading up to the entrance, nodding to the armed skeleton sentries stationed along the stairs. When they arrived at the top of the temple, a pair of skeleton guards brought them deep within the heart of the temple to the lair of the Skeleton King. There, the king sat on a throne at the center of this throne room—still wearing his crown of finger bones and still stroking his long beard. All around him sat his generals and other high-ranking skeletons. Bacca couldn't help but think how much the skeletons' throne room looked like the zombies' throne room in Gravehome. Maybe these two mobs had more in common than they thought.

"What is the news?" the Skeleton King asked, rising from his throne. "Is the matter taken care of?"

"We don't have the Bonesword yet, if that's what you mean," Bacca answered. "But we know who took it, and I *think* we know where it is now."

Bacca told the king about his interrogation of the guards at Rotpit, the visit to the witches' hut, and what he and Dug had heard about the Fortress of Confusion.

"Now you face quite a challenge," the Skeleton King said. "The Fortress of Confusion is a dangerous place. You will need to be very careful."

"I've never heard of this fortress before," Bacca said. "And I've heard of practically every fortress around. What can you tell me about it?"

"For one, my brother lives there," the Skeleton King explained. "Thousands of years ago, he and I were the final two candidates to become the next Skeleton King—this was after the old king died bravely fighting an Ender Dragon. Some skeletons said he shouldn't have been shooting arrows at an Ender Dragon in the first place, but that is neither here nor there. Anyhow, after a fiercely-fought contest, I was selected to be the new king. My brother had wanted the job very much, and so he angrily stormed off to the stone beach biome and shut himself inside the Fortress of Confusion. In the many years since, he has never returned. He is a very strange man."

"I see," said Bacca. "What else can you tell us about the Fortress of Confusion? Why does it have that name?"

"First of all, it's very old," the Skeleton King said. "It predates construction of this temple by several thousand years. It is named the Fortress of Confusion because those who enter through its single door describe of a maze of confounding tricks and traps unlike any fortress the Overworld has ever seen. Very few have ventured beyond the first room. Some who have tried to solve its mysteries have never come back again. None have reached the center of the fortress and returned to tell their tale."

"Tricks and traps?" Bacca said with a confident smile. "Sounds like my kind of place."

"There is more," cautioned the Skeleton King. "The Fortress of Confusion is also said to be magic. Some skeletons even believe it is somehow . . . *aware*. Those who have returned often report the sensation of being watched while inside. Some even claim the fortress moves by itself. They say that when they reenter a room, the things inside of it are changed. Over the years, it has become difficult to know what is fact and what is fiction about the place. So many conflicting stories are told. The original purpose of the fortress may be forever lost to history. The only thing that seems certain now is that something powerful and mysterious lies within."

The Skeleton King stood up and walked to the far side of the throne room. The other skeletons moved out of his way. Against the wall was a very old dresser. Bacca saw that unlike most dressers—which were made with stacked planks and trap doors—this one had been made with bones. The Skeleton King pulled on the lid. The bony hinges creaked and the top opened. The Skeleton King looked inside.

"This is the only other aid I can give you," the king said. He reached into the dresser and pulled something out, then strode back to Bacca and Dug. The generals and skeleton dignitaries looked in awe at what the king carried. (If they'd had eyes, they would have been bulging out of their heads.)

The king appeared to be clutching a large tablet of dark prismarine—though maybe it was just regular prismarine that had gone dark over the ages. It looked very, very, *very* old. The closer it got, the older it looked. It might have been the oldest material Bacca had ever seen.

"This is the Tablet of Mystery," the Skeleton King said reverently. "It is one of our most sacred artifacts. It is believed to have been crafted by whatever race of ancient skeletons built the Fortress of Confusion. There is a legend that says the tablet holds keys for safe passage through the fortress, but no skeleton has ever been able to decipher its markings definitively. Perhaps you can, and perhaps it will aid you on your journey. Place it in your inventory and guard it well."

Several of the skeletons put their bony hands to their mouths. They were stunned. The king was handing over one of their most important historical objects to an outsider.

The king, sensing this astonishment, quickly added: "And we expect it back, in one piece, when your journey is concluded!"

"Of course," Bacca said.

He carefully took the prismarine tablet from the king. At first, he thought he must be holding it upside down, because it just looked like a bunch of jagged markings that made no sense. Then he turned it around. Then he tried another angle. And another. But no matter how Bacca held the tablet, it still remained unreadable.

The Skeleton King noticed Bacca's frustration.

"Generations of skeletons have tried to decode the writing on it," said the king. "Not one has ever been successful. I hope you will succeed where others have failed. From what I hear, you have a reputation for cleverness."

Bacca shrugged and put the prismarine block into his inventory. He would give it a closer inspection later.

"Thanks," Bacca said to the king. "I'm sure this will help. I actually came here to ask one more favor. I have no idea how long it will take us to find the Bonesword once we're in the fortress. I'm hoping that the zombies will not immediately start fighting again once the truce is over. Can I expect the same from you skeletons?"

The Skeleton King stroked his long beard and shook his head.

"I have a responsibility to protect my people," he said. "That is the first duty of a king, and I intend to do my duty. If we are attacked, I must order my warriors to defend themselves."

"But you won't, like, strike first?" Bacca pressed.

The Skeleton King was clearly not used to being challenged on his military policy. Generally, Bacca didn't like to make people uncomfortable, but he felt like he had to in this situation. There was so much at stake.

"Fine," the Skeleton King said reluctantly. "You have my word. We will not strike first. But I can't I promise anything more than that. If the zombies attack us, we will fight back."

Bacca decided this was probably the most he could hope for. He thanked the king for his help, and shook the king's bony hand. (It felt weird, like shaking a handful of dice.)

"It is *we* who should thank *you*," said the king. "If you retrieve the Bonesword and stop this war, many skeletons will be saved. Also, if you happen to see my brother . . . please, tell him no hard feelings."

"Will do," agreed Bacca.

The Skeleton King gave Bacca and Dug a special detachment of skeleton warriors who led them through the jungle and out to the stone beach biome. From there, it was easy to find the entrance to the Fortress of Confusion. It was at the bottom of an immense cliff, and the top of the cliff was carved into the shape of a skull.

"Good luck, fellas," said the leader of the skeleton warriors as he turned to go. He marched his detachment back toward the jungle in a hurry. It was clear the skeletons did not like being around this place.

The entrance to the Fortress of Confusion was framed by a circle of bedrock blocks. There was no door, simply a large opening. Past the opening, a dark passageway led into unseen depths beyond.

It was a scary-looking for sure, but Bacca had seen scarier.

Then he wondered . . . what about his student?

"Dug, I realize this is more than you signed up for when you enrolled in a summer crafting class," Bacca said as they peered into the dark entrance. "I don't know exactly what we're going to encounter inside this place, but it will probably involve risk and peril.."

"mmmm*And* confusion, judging by the name," Dug pointed out.

"Yes," said Bacca. "That too. Anyway, you don't have to come if you don't want to."

"mmmm*I* want to," said Dug. "Don't forget, I'm a zombie as well as a crafter. I want this war to stop too."

"Good," said Bacca. "In that case, let's go find out what's inside!"

And they walked through the dark opening that led into the fortress.

CHAPTER TEN

Flappy cruised through the sky, coasting on a warm, pleasant zephyr. He was glad to be rid of that long sharp bone he'd been carrying, and even more glad to be headed *away* from the scary cliff with the grabby skeleton hand. The witches might be grumpy most of the time, but at least they never snatched things out of his claws without asking. Apparently, skeleton hands could be quite rude.

The biome where the witches lived came into view. Flappy realized that he had never been so happy to return home. As the familiar witches' hut on chicken legs appeared, a great surprise was waiting for him.

Flappy had never seen a creature so large or so magnificent. Its coat was ruffled gently by the same breeze that carried Flappy through the skies. Its eyes were like redstone, and infused with a supernatural fire. The witches had gathered at the front of their hut and were talking to the enormous wolf through their doorway. The wolf was so tall that it hardly needed to stretch to reach the door of the hut.

As Flappy drew closer, the curiosity he was feeling quickly turned to concern. Flappy saw expressions of overwhelming pleasure on the faces of the witches. This was cause for concern because the witches were usually only pleased by *horrible* things. Flappy had seen these same expressions before, like the time when the witches totally vaporized a cow with an especially powerful potion. Or when they made a particularly tasty stew out of a group of villagers. Or when they saw a rabbit fall into a hole where it couldn't get out again. (Flappy had to go back later, after the witches had left, and help it escape).

The wolf was big, that much was clear, but it didn't look dangerous, let alone particularly horrible. So why were the witches so pleased?

The grinning witches and the wolf were talking to each other (not only was this wolf particular large, but it could also speak!?), and the wolf's answers looked like they pleased the witches immensely. Their smiles got even bigger. All of this made Flappy increasingly nervous.

While the witches were distracted with the wolf, Flappy flew in through the window at the rear of the hut. There he waited and listened to the conversation. At first, Flappy did not understand . . . there was something about plans for zombies. Flappy had heard the witches chatter on this topic before. The witches were jealous of the zombies. Not about the moaning and eating people raw, of course. Those were all things witches naturally considered themselves to be *above*. But the witches were envious of what the zombies *had*. Gravehome, specifically. A hut—even a hut that stood up high on really cool chicken legs—was still no match for a luxurious mountain fortress.

Then Flappy remembered he had heard the witches talk about a deal they would make one day.

A deal that would let them have their own fortress. A place like Gravehome.

As Flappy continued to look back and forth between the gleeful witches and the enormous wolf (just one of his incisor teeth was bigger than all of Flappy!), another idea began to occur to him. A quite scary idea indeed. The more Flappy listened, the more certain he became.

Something was about to happen. Something very, very big. And it would change everything.

CHAPTER ELEVEN

"**M**mmm*I* wonder what this place was originally," Dug said. "Like, when it was built, and what was it built *for*? Those were things the Skeleton King either couldn't tell us . . . or didn't want to."

Bacca and Dug slowly made their way down the dark hallway that led inside the Fortress of Confusion. The way ahead was lit only by the torches they carried, and the solitary sound they could hear was their own footsteps.

"mmmm*I* also wonder what kind of tools crafters used back in those days," Dug continued. Bacca noticed with pride that the young crafter's mind was always working, always questioning. A promising sign of good things to come.

"I bet they used the same ones we have today," Bacca answered. "The trick to knowing what tools someone used is to look at what they crafted. I expect we'll understand more when we see what's up ahead. Whatever *that* is . . . "

Dug nodded seriously. They proceeded further down the corridor.

Soon, the pathway ahead began to widen. The walls held sconces with torches in them. Bacca lit them with his own torch as they walked past. Soon, the tunnel was full of light.

The corridor widened even more and opened into a large room. At first, both Bacca and Dug were unsure what it might be. It was a very strange place.

The floor was made of blocks of standstone, and there were several rows of red standstone benches. Past the benches was a raised, flat area of grey andesite—like a large platform. Behind the platform on the far wall was what seemed to be a mural, made from many different blocks, including bright blue lapis lazuli, which made the room feel almost like it was underwater.

To the right and left of the platform were doors made of polished granite. The one on the left had not been opened in some time. It was covered with dust. The door on the right was another matter entirely. It looked as though someone had once cut through it with an axe, and it had been rebuilt many times. Disturbingly, there were bones scattered near it—whether from skeletons or other sources, Bacca could not immediately tell. It was clear that someone, or some*thing,* had hoped to keep anyone from passing through it. To Bacca's trained eye, it looked like it had recently been crafted shut from the other side.

"Well this is a weird one," Bacca said, holding his torch high to take it all in.

Dug walked over to the bones that littered the ground near the rebuilt door. He carefully picked them up and turned them over in his hands.

"mmmm*None* of these are the Bonesword," Dug said sadly. "Or any kind of sword."

"I could have told you that," Bacca said. "It looks like they're the bones of folks who tried to get through that door. It's probably trapped. I say we *don't* go that way."

"mmmm*I* agree," Dug said.

"Something about this place feels familiar to me, but I can't quite put my finger on it," said Bacca. "Let's look around for more clues."

Bacca and Dug explored the room. Bacca approached the door to the left and ran his claws around its dusty edges. Then he pushed it. No dice. It seemed to be locked. Dug found a small stone staircase that led from the floor of the room up to the top of the platform. He climbed up, and, standing on the platform, realized something.

"mmmm*This* is a stage!" he announced to Bacca.

Bacca took a look. Dug was right.

"It sure *is* a stage," Bacca answered. "And all these rows of benches out front . . . they're for an audience. You could put on a show here. Or a play. I *thought* something was familiar about this room. It's a theater! Hmmm. I wonder what kind of plays ancient skeletons liked to watch. I bet they involved lots of arrow shooting."

For a moment, both Bacca and Dug scanned the ornate, colorful backdrop at the back of the stage, looking for clues.

"mmmm*It* looks like *Zombies of the Coast*," Dug said, then added, "But that doesn't make any sense. Must be a coincidence."

"*Zombies of the Coast*?" Bacca asked. "What's that?"

"mmmm*It's* a play," Dug replied. "It's by William De Kay, the most famous zombie playwright. We have to learn it in school. This backdrop with all the lapis lazuli blocks—it looks like the ocean backdrop for that play. The sandstone blocks along the bottom make a coastline, and those blocks of emerald look like potatoes growing. *Zombies of the Coast* is about some zombies who have their potatoes stolen by a very tricky sheep. They have to chase the sheep away."

"Now, to me, that sounds an awfully lot like *Skeletons of the Coast*," Bacca said.

"mmmm*What*?" said Dug suspiciously. "That's not a thing. Is it?"

"Sure it is," Bacca answered. "It's a skeleton play. I don't know it that well, but the plot involves everything you just described. Except instead of zombies, it's skeletons. And instead of a sheep trying to steal potatoes, it's a cow trying to steal carrots. The play is supposed to date from the origins of skeleton history."

"mmmm*Maybe* it . . . influenced William De Kay," Dug said.

"Maybe so," Bacca said with a grin.

Bacca and Dug explored the backdrop of the stage with its coastline design. They searched for any hidden doors or openings that would allow them to move beyond the theater, but found nothing. Bacca noticed that his student was starting to look downtrodden. He realized that Dug had never faced a challenge like this.

"mmmm*I'm* beginning to feel frustrated," Dug said, as if reading Bacca's thoughts. "There are only two doors out of this room. The one to the right is crafted shut and looks booby-trapped, probably by the Skeleton King's brother—or maybe even by the fortress itself. And the door to the left is locked and sealed, maybe magically. I don't see a way forward."

"Now now, don't go getting discouraged just yet," Bacca said. "I know. Maybe we should try looking at that tablet the Skeleton King gave us."

"mmmm*Okay*," Dug said. "Let's give it a try."

Bacca carefully took the Tablet of Mystery out of his inventory and placed it at the foot of the stage. Bacca and Dug crowded around the ancient pris-marine block and looked for any clues it might contain. It was filled with confusing dots and squiggles. Bacca and Dug strained to make sense of them.

After a moment, Dug said, "mmmm*What* about those dots over there?"

He pointed his greenish zombie finger at a corner of the tablet.

"What about them?" Bacca asked.

"mmmm*There's* three small ones, and one big one," Dug said. "The three small ones could be zombies, and the big one could be a sheep. And look at these little notches between them. Those could be potatoes."

Bacca thought Dug might be onto something.

"Or it could also be showing us the positions of skeletons, a cow, and some carrots," Bacca said. "Maybe it means we're supposed to *put on* the play."

Dug looked up at Bacca like he couldn't believe he was serious.

"Don't worry about having stage fright," Bacca said warmly. "It's completely normal before a big show. Besides, there isn't even an audience—not that I can see, anyway."

"mmmm*But* there are only two of us," Dug objected. "For the play, we need three zombies and a sheep."

"First of all, I think we ought to do the skeleton play, seeing as we're in a skeleton venue," Bacca gently suggested, careful not to accidentally offend Dug, who might have a sentimental attachment to the zombie version.

"mmmm*Fine*," Dug said. "Then three skeletons and a cow. It's still two more characters than we have actors."

"I think we can find a way around that," Bacca said.

"mmmm*How?*" asked Dug.

"I'm willing to bet that a couple of skilled crafters like us could *make* some skeletons and cows in a pinch," Bacca said.

Dug's expression changed. He clearly liked the sound of this. Being an actor was one thing, but *crafting* actors was quite another.

They got to work.

Bacca took out his favorite diamond pickaxe and started mining slabs of sandstone from the blocks that made up the theater's floor. Then he chipped them down until they were almost sandstone sticks. After that he cut notches into the ends so that they would fit together like bones.

When he had a bigpile of these "bones" he took them up to the stage and began assembling them into figures that looked a whole lot like three large skeletons trying to guard some carrots.

Bacca glanced over and saw that Dug was also crafting something. After a moment, Bacca realized that it was not, as he'd assumed, a cow. Instead, Dug was taking iron ingots out of his inventory and combining them with wooden sticks. Before long, Dug had several feet of track stacked beside him. Then he took stacks of iron ingots and crafted them into minecarts.

"mmmm*Here*," Dug said, positioning the tracks across the stage. "This way, our skeletons can move around. We can put them on minecarts and push them. They'll need to start beside the water, then move across the stage to chase the sheep—I mean, cow—away from the potatoes—I mean, carrots."

"Nice!" Bacca said. "I was thinking we would have to move the skeleton statues by hand. This will be much better!"

Bacca helped Dug lay the track across the stage, and then placed the skeletons in the minecarts.

"mmmm*Whee!*" Dug said, pushing one of the minecarts. The skeleton glided effortlessly across the stage.

"Not so fast," said Bacca. "The play hasn't even started yet! Our skeletons don't even have bows. Everyone knows that a skeleton without a bow is like a . . . like a . . . um. Anyhow, it's like something really lousy."

They combined sticks and strings to make bows for the skeletons. When that was completed, they prepared to craft the cow.

"mmmm*It* should be an *evil-looking* cow," insisted Dug. "It's trying to steal from the skeletons. It's the bad guy."

"Okay," Bacca said. "We'll give it big hairy eyebrows that are arched like it's feeling mean."

Dug thought this was a good idea.

Cows were basically black and white. Bacca took some more sandstone out of the floor, and used it to make the whiter parts of the animal. Then, he took a few blocks of coal out of his inventory and made the cow's dark spots and mean-looking eyebrows. Dug and Bacca lifted the cow into a waiting minecart. Then they carefully placed the minecart onto the tracks.

"Let's see how it looks from out there," Bacca said. He jumped off the stage and dashed into the seats. He crept all around the theater, looking at their creations from every perspective. If he squinted his eyes just right, Bacca could believe he was really standing by a beach watching a cow sneak up on some skeletons.

Dug joined Bacca at the back of the theater.

"mmmm*It* looks good to me," Dug said. "But I don't even know who our audience is. Like, who will be watching? There's nobody here."

Bacca headed back up to the stage.

"In my somewhat limited experience with magic, it's a good idea to assume that someone is *always* watching," Bacca replied. "Now let's give the people—er, well, I suppose I mean, the magic—what it came to see."

Bacca positioned himself behind the skeletons, and Dug stood so he could operate the evil cow. Together, they used the figures they had crafted to stage a production of *Skeletons of the Coast*.

Both Bacca and Dug were familiar with the basics of the story. First, the cow sneaks up on the skeletons and knocks them over when they're not looking. To accomplish this, Dug rolled the cow statue on the minecart until it collided with the skeletons. Bacca ensured the skeletons bounced around dramatically and fell over. Dug maneuvered the cow so that it seemed to steal the emerald green carrot tops built into the background. Then the skeletons collected themselves—sometimes literally, as some bones had been dislodged during the collision—and proceeded to chase the cow around the stage for most of the rest of the play. Dug had built a circular track for this. Dug and Bacca had fun pushing the skeletons so that they never quite caught up to the cow.

"mmmm*This* acting business is hard work," the tiny zombie whispered as he huffed and puffed behind the cow statue.

"Shhhh," Bacca whispered back. "Don't break character. That's the first rule of acting."

"mmmm*Oh*, right," said Dug. "Sorry."

They pushed the figures around the stage some more. Bacca knew that ancient skeleton plays were big on action and short on dialogue. Or really any plot development beyond one thing trying to catch, shoot, or eat another thing. (Seeing as how this was what most skeletons spent all their time thinking about, plays that had a lot of these things were usually crowd-pleasers.)

Eventually, Bacca decided they'd had enough action—even for a skeleton play—and got ready to wrap things up.

"Okay," Bacca whispered to Dug. "It's time for the denouement and happy ending."

"mmmm*The* day-new-what?" Dug whispered, scratching his head. "That sounds like something you'd accidentally step in."

"It means the part of the play after the fun, chasing part," Bacca answered.

"mmmm*Oh* . . . you mean the boring part right before the end?" Dug said.

"Yes, exactly," said Bacca.

Bacca and Dug manipulated their creations so that the cow suddenly stopped in its tracks. The skeletons in hot pursuit ran into the cow, then ran into each other, then fell down again. The cow used this as an opportunity to put the carrots back in the ground, and then run away offstage. The skeletons slowly got back up and found that their carrots had been returned. Then they celebrated and jumped around. Then the play was over.

"mmmm*I* don't think skeletons even *like* carrots," Dug whispered as he and Bacca walked to the center of the stage and took a bow.

"That's called 'artistic license,'" Bacca said. "It means you can do anything you want, if it's for a play."

"mmmm*Oh,*" Dug said, taking a second bow. "That's certainly convenient."

It felt strange to take bows in an empty theater without anybody applauding, but Bacca felt like it might be an important part of the production. He smiled and pretended there was an audience of skeletons clapping their bony hands and stomping their bony feet for more.

After they had taken several rounds of bows, Bacca and Dug left the stage by the stone stairs on the side. For a moment, there was an eerie silence in the theater. Bacca and Dug both looked intently at the magically sealed door.

Nothing happened.

At first.

Then, just as Dug opened his mouth to say he thought it hadn't worked (only getting as far as "mmmm"), there was a strange grating sound, like blocks of sandstone grinding hard against other blocks of sandstone. As the crafters looked on, the sealed door began to open by itself. Dust that had not moved for centuries was shaken away. The door swung wide, and a mysterious hallway was revealed beyond. They had done it!

"mmmm*I* can't believe that worked!" said Dug. "Wow. This is awesome!"

"When you've been doing this as long as I have, you get good at telling which doors might open magically," Bacca said. "That same experience also tells me that where you encounter one magical door, you're likely to encounter more."

"mmmm*Gee*, what a crazy place," Dug said.

"Let's go down that corridor that just opened up," Bacca said, heading for it. "I'm willing to bet this fortress is going to get a whole lot crazier."

CHAPTER TWELVE

Drooler hid behind the hill until the patrol of skeletons marched past. He had never been this deep into skeleton territory. Heck, he had never been this far from Gravehome. For all of his ambition and desire for power, Drooler was, fundamentally, a zombie who liked to stick close to home. He liked to be indoors. He didn't enjoy going outside, even for very important things . . . like plotting with witches.

Plotting with witches . . .

That, Drooler reflected, was what had led to his current predicament. Now he was farther from home than he ever had been, dodging patrols of skeletons with dangerous-looking bows, and looking for a way out of the hole he'd dug himself into (and of all the holes a zombie could find oneself in, it had to be the *one* bad one!).

Why, wondered Drooler, did things never prove to be as easy as you thought they were going to be?

Drooler was a born coward. Since his earliest days, he had always run away from danger whenever possible. Even in his evil dealings as an adult, he had found that getting people to do dangerous things for him was always preferable to doing them personally. During his rise to power in the zombie court, Drooler had paid bribes to other zombies to carry out intrigues against his enemies. He never lifted a finger—his own, or someone else's—when he could help it.

Other times, Drooler used tricks to undo his enemies that didn't involve other zombies at all. These were the best because they were the least risky. Nobody could squeal. Once, he gave a frenemy a watch for his undead birthday that always lied about how much time there was before the sun came back up. Another time, he left a treasure map on another opponent's desk, and let him "discover" that it led you to a pit from which you could never escape. Oh how Drooler loved these evil inventions!

But Drooler's problem now was that he had to do things all on his own. The zombies back at Gravehome couldn't help him. The witches couldn't help him. He had nobody left to manipulate. For once in his afterlife, he was going to have to fix things himself.

When the skeleton patrol passed out of sight, Drooler moved out of his hiding place and pressed even deeper into the skeleton-filled jungle. . . .

CHAPTER THIRTEEN

Bacca and Dug carefully walked down the corridor leading away from the auditorium. They
reached a corner and rounded it, and began
to see a dim light up ahead. A few hundred feet up
the hallway was a room. Something was illuminat-
ing it from the inside.

"mmmm*Glowstones*," said Dug. "Only they
make that kind of light. Must be imported all the
way from the Nether. How fancy."

"Yeah," said Bacca. "This fortress is clearly old,
but the Nether is way older. And light from glowstones never goes out."

Bacca and Dug walked toward the light until
they reached an open doorway. The room beyond
had a high ceiling with—sure enough—glowstones
set into the corners, and a floor of plain cobblestone. Dominating the room was a large chair—
with a tall, high back—made out of the darkest
black obsidian. Seated on the throne was what
appeared to be an obsidian skeleton. Upon closer
inspection by Bacca and Dug, it was revealed to be
only a *statue* of a skeleton. Except for the material, it was nearly identical to the ones that Bacca

and Dug had crafted for their play in the previous chamber. Clearly they had done a good job.

"Whoever crafted this, we're at least as good as they were," Bacca said confidently.

Dug poked the obsidian skeleton to see if it would move. Much to his relief, it didn't. It was just a sculpture.

At the top of the tall chair above the skeleton was a simple tablet of red sandstone. There was strange writing on the tablet. The letters looked like bones.

On the north wall—opposite the corridor where Bacca and Dug had entered the room—there was another door. Bacca ran his paw over it, and gave it a tap with his diamond axe. Just as he'd suspected, it was magically sealed. Nobody had opened it in a very long time.

There was a final, confusing element to the room: a few feet in front of the skeleton was a big pile of broken blocks and crafting components. Most of these blocks were—or had once been—sandstone. There were also bones, blocks of diamond, blocks of emerald, gold and iron ingots, and even pieces of armor. Bacca and Dug sifted through this pile of rubble, looking for clues. It had once been a structure of some kind, but had fallen apart a very long time ago.

"mmmm*This* is a strange room," Dug said, tossing a broken block of emerald back into the pile. "I wonder why this skeleton is sitting here looking at this pile of junk."

"Agreed," said Bacca. "It's a mystery to me as well. I also wonder what we have to do to get that door to open. It's clearly sealed by magic."

"mmmm*Could* it want to see another play?" Dug suggested.

"That sounds too easy," Bacca replied, scratching his furry chin as he thought.

"mmmm*Maybe* we should begin with that funny writing at the top of the skeleton's chair," Dug suggested, pointing over to the obsidian throne. "Can you read it?"

"Actually, I can," Bacca said, approaching the seated figure. "My Ancient Skeleton isn't what it used to be, but I think it says something like 'Time Traveler.'"

"mmmm*Time* Traveler?" Dug said. "Really?"

Bacca nodded. That was what the bony letters spelled out. Or so it looked to Bacca.

"mmmm*That's* silly," Dug said without hesitation. "Everybody knows you can't travel through time. If you could, then you go back in time and save the life of the person you used to be before you became a zombie. So then you wouldn't ever become a zombie. But then you couldn't go back in time and save yourself. And so . . . and so . . . after that, it gets pretty darn confusing."

Bacca laughed.

"I agree with you," he said. "But I think to solve this puzzle we've got to keep an open mind."

Something occurred to Dug.

"mmmm*You* don't think that this pile of stuff on the ground . . . used to *be* some kind of *time machine*?!" Dug sputtered.

"No," said Bacca. "I mean . . . *probably* not."

Dug looked even more confused.

" . . . but why don't we see if the Tablet of Mystery has anything to say," Bacca quickly finished.

They took the strange tablet out of Bacca's inventory and began scanning it for clues. They carefully checked on both sides, turning it over and over, again and again, hunting for anything that looked like it could be related to the obsidian chair or time travel.

"mmmm*I* don't see a time machine," Dug said. "Though maybe that's because I don't know what one looks like."

Bacca nodded. He had seen many things in his adventures across the Overworld, but a time machine wasn't one of them.

"mmmm*But* look at this," Dug said, suddenly interested in an image in one corner of the tablet. "That thing with little slashes on top of an 'L' could be a skeleton sitting in a chair."

Bacca looked closely at where Dug was pointing. If he squinted his eyes and turned his head to the side, he had to admit . . . the ancient etchings kind of *did* look like the reclining obsidian skeleton.

"You might have something here, Dug," Bacca said.

"mmmm*So* if that's the skeleton, then what's this?" Dug asked, pointing to the spot on the tablet just in front of the reclining bones. "It looks like a tiny house. Or hut. Or . . . or . . ."

"A booth," Bacca said knowingly.

"mmmm*Yes*," Dug agreed, nodding. "I suppose it could be a little booth, too."

Bacca was suddenly one hundred percent certain.

"I've heard of these things," Bacca explained. "Apparently, many years ago, ancient skeletons used to build little booths everywhere. There haven't been any for a long time, though. Skeleton architecture styles have totally changed."

"mmmm*Were* they like toll booths?" Dug asked. "Where you have to pay money to walk down a road? I've seen those before. They're really simple. Just a tiny square house with a window. Any beginner could craft one. But why would skeletons have toll booths?"

"I don't think they were for collecting money," Bacca answered. "I suspect they were a way for skeletons to quickly duck out of the sun. Skeletons could use them in emergencies if they lost track of time and suddenly the sun came up. This was before they invented living in temples."

"mmmm*That* makes sense," Dug said thoughtfully. "I've heard that my own ancestors—ancient zombies—did some strange things too. But we don't talk about them in public. The skeletons could find out."

"So here's an idea," Bacca said. "What if our job is to build the skeleton booth out of the heap of stuff on the floor? What if our bony friend is a time traveler because our doing this will let him go back in time—because he'll be seeing things the way they used to be?"

"mmmm*That's* a good idea," said Dug.

"Yeah . . ." said Bacca, suddenly becoming more cautious. "The problem is that neither of us has ever seen an ancient skeleton booth. Probably no living crafter has. So we're going to have to hope we're very good at guessing."

Bacca and Dug began through the pile of crafting materials. Most of the sandstone was still salvageable. Bacca and Dug began working with these blocks first, using them to create sandstone slabs and smooth sandstone.

"From what I've heard, these skeleton booths were small and circular," Bacca told Dug. "They weren't too high, either. Not much taller than a skeleton."

It wasn't much to work from, but based on this description, Dug got started crafting. He thought about what kind of booth a skeleton would find useful if dawn snuck up. The booth would have to have an entrance that was easy to see, he decided, so Dug used the decorative emerald, gold, and diamond blocks to frame the doorway clearly. He made the walls out of sandstone and gave it a simple, flat roof. This used up most of the crafting materials from the pile, but there were still a few old pieces of armor scattered around. It was all different types of armor, and none of it could be combined to form a matching set. Dug placed these bits of armor inside the booth like they were decorations. (Bacca also did not have a better idea for where they should go.)

When he was done, Dug stepped back from his creation and took a look. So did Bacca.

"mmmm*So* . . ." Dug began, "does it look like a skeleton booth from back in ancient times?"

"I mean . . . I *think* it does," Bacca said. "At least, it looks like it *could be* one."

"mmmm*Then* the door should open and allow us to pass through, right?" Dug said. "Like, right about . . . now?" Bacca could tell Dug was growing impatient. The door in question had not budged even an inch.

The crafters waited and watched. Nothing happened.

"Did we do something wrong?" Bacca wondered. "I know we're guessing, but I think this was a really good guess."

Both crafters paced around the room, trying to figure out what to do next. Both considered the possibility that they had missed a clue . . . but what?

They searched high and low for anything else that might tell them how to proceed.

Then Dug said: "mmmm*Wait* a minute. I just thought of something. This obsidian skeleton was crafted back when the Fortress of Confusion was built, right? Back in the day, when there were still ancient skeleton booths."

"Yes," Bacca said. "This fortress was built many thousands of years ago. That's what the Skeleton King told us."

"mmmm*Well* why would it be 'time traveling' for this obsidian skeleton to see something that was *already around when he was*? It wouldn't."

Bacca thought that Dug had a valid point.

"mmmm*What* if instead of travelling *backwards* in time, this skeleton wants to travel *forward*?"

Bacca saw where Dug was going, and liked it.

"So, instead of showing him something from the days of ancient skeletons—his own time—we should show him what skeleton temples look like today?" said Bacca.

"mmmm*Yes*," Dug said. "For him, that would be the distant future."

This plan made a lot of sense to Bacca. The crafting materials that skeletons used over the ages had never really changed, they had just been used to craft different things. Like temples. Skeleton styles had evolved, but the crafting components hadn't.

"Okay," Bacca said, "we can totally do this. We're going to be a little tight on materials, but that's okay. Something tells me we can still make it work."

Bacca and Dug carefully took their booth apart and started all over again, from scratch. They built a large square floor for the temple, then used the remaining blocks to form a pyramid that gradually rose out of the base. Because they had so few sandstone blocks, Bacca and Dug could only make one small central room. Into this room they placed the remaining emerald and diamond blocks, as well as the strange assortment of armor.

"mmmm*If* I saw this out in a jungle somewhere, I'd say it was the smallest skeleton temple of all time," Dug observed as they put the final block in place.

"I would too," Bacca said. "But it would still count as a skeleton temple. I think that's the important part."

Bacca and Dug took several steps back from their creation, so that the time traveler could have an unobstructed view. Bacca had no idea if the jet-black figure on the throne was "alive" in any sense, or just a tool of the fortress. What had the Skeleton King said about the fortress itself being aware? Thinking about that made Bacca feel just a little creeped-out and scared. Because of this, he jumped when a loud and sudden grinding sound began to emanate from the wall behind them. Bacca and Dug turned around and saw the magically-sealed door opening under its own power.

"mmmm*We* did it!" shouted Dug, leaping a foot into the air. "I'm jumping for joy."

"Yes we did," Bacca said. "Incidentally, that's why I was jumping too. The joy."

Bacca and Dug gathered their crafting tools and prepared to head to whatever might be beyond the newly-opened doorway.

"I'm glad that you thought of time traveling *forward* in time," Bacca said. "Nicely done."

"mmmm*I* think it was just beginner's luck," Dug said humbly.

BACCA AND THE SKELETON KING   127

"I don't know about that," Bacca said. "Keep up the good work, kid."

Leaving the strange obsidian skeleton behind, they passed through the doorway, and into a new place where an even greater challenge waited.

CHAPTER FOURTEEN

The Skeleton King had dealt with his share of memorable crises over the years. A critical shortage of arrows. Unexpected aggression from a horde of angry cave spiders. And, now, an unprovoked attack by the zombies from Gravehome.

As king, it was his responsibility to solve each and every problem that happened under his rule. Having been at the job for many years, the king had learned that problems like these were typically solved with obvious solutions. Opening up arrow stockpiles and cracking down on arrow-hoarding. Making sure cave spiders understood the difference between mine shafts and skeleton temples. These solutions had always worked.

But this new problem with the zombies . . . The more he tried to fix it, the more complicated it got. And now—somehow—all hope for resolving it peacefully rested on a hairy crafter and his young zombie student.

Given all the weird things that were happening, the Skeleton King was not really that surprised when his man-at-arms barged into the throne room with a confused look on his skull.

"Yes?" chattered the king.

"Your highness, we've captured a zombie," said the man-at-arms. "Some of our soldiers caught him trying to sneak inside this temple."

"Sneaking in *here*?" the king asked. "For what purpose? Doesn't he know there's a truce? Was he aggressive? Was he armed?"

"No," said the man-at-arms. "Nothing like that. When we asked why he was here, he said he wanted to talk to *you*."

For a moment, the king felt hopeful.

"Is he an emissary from Gravehome?" the Skeleton King asked.

Perhaps the zombies had sent someone to nego-tiate an end to the fighting. For a moment, the Skeleton King dared to dream.

"No," the man-at-arms answered. "He says he came on his own."

The king slumped back into his throne. At any other time, he would have sent a zombie like this—who was obviously crazy—away without a second thought. But these were *not* other times. These were crazy times. These were times that called for extreme measures. Like seeing what visiting zom-bies—even ones who had not bothered to make an appointment—had to say.

"Send him in," said the Skeleton King.

"Your highness . . . are you serious?" said the man-at-arms. "We only thought we should tell you about him because we thought you might have some preference as to the *way* he was executed."

"That won't be necessary," said the king. "Just bring him to me."

Astounded, the man-at-arms left and returned with three skeleton soldiers marching in a tri-angle. In the center of the triangle was a very unhappy looking zombie in diamond armor. The skeletons had tied his arms with ropes. Each of the skeleton soldiers kept one hand on its bow, ready to draw and fire if the zombie made any wrong moves.

The man-at-arms signaled to the zombie that he should approach the king. The zombie walked up slowly, his eyes scanning the corners of the room, hoping to see a friendly face but finding none.

"A zombie risking almost certain death by sneaking into this temple . . . to talk to *me*?" said the king. "Now I really have seen everything. So, what do you have to ask me, Mister Zombie?"

"Mmmm*Drooler* is my name, actually," the zombie said. "And I have something important to tell you. It's a matter of state secrecy. It's top-secret. Top-*top*-secret. So secret in fact that I don't think I should tell you where other people can hear."

His arms were tied, so Drooler used his feet to gesture toward the soldiers and the man-at-arms.

"Very well," said the king. "Man-at-arms, you and your men please step to the far side of the room, out of earshot. If this zombie makes one false move—or acts aggressive in the slightest—please shoot him in the back as quickly as you can."

"With pleasure," said the man-at-arms, nocking an arrow in his bow.

Drooler let out a nervous "gulp."

When the other skeletons had moved away, the Skeleton King whispered, "Drooler . . . I have heard that name before. Bacca believes you were the one who started this war in the first place. Give me one good reason why I shouldn't tell my guards to fire their arrows right now."

"mmmm*Something* even more horrible is about to happen . . . if it hasn't happened already," said Drooler.

"More horrible than an unnecessary war?" the Skeleton King said skeptically. "What in the Overworld could that be?"

Drooler nervously looked left and right, as if afraid the crevasses in the blocks around him might hear the next thing he had to say.

"mmmm*The* Spirit of the Taiga," said Drooler with a tremor in his voice.

"Oh?" the Skeleton King said, sounding relieved. "Is that all? I know the Spirit of the Taiga. Giant wolfy fellow. Likes to receive gifts. Also likes to eat people, as I recall. Consequently, he doesn't receive many gifts."

"mmmm*Well,* let's just say that he received a gift he really, *really* likes from some witches," said Drooler, careful to omit the fact that he had been the one to deliver said gift. "The Spirit of the Taiga liked his gift so much, he's agreed to do a favor for the witches. A favor that will be very bad for us."

"Which is . . . ?" the Skeleton King asked impatiently. He cast an annoyed look at his man-at-arms. Behind him, Drooler could hear bowstrings straining.

"mmmm*The* Spirit of the Taiga has agreed to clear the zombies out of Gravehome so that the witches can have it," Drooler said, a mask of terror upon his face. "He's powerful enough to do it, too. They may hold him off for a while, but eventually he will be able to tunnel his way inside. Once he does that, the zombies will have no defense. And once he gives Gravehome to the witches, the zombies will be homeless."

"You'll forgive me for not crying a river of tears," said the Skeleton King sarcastically. "I could do that if I had eyes and tear ducts, you know. But these are the same zombies that have been attacking my people! Lots of skeletons don't like the zombies right now. Some of them—I'm not saying me—might even be *happy* that The Spirit of the Taiga was doing this."

"mmmm*But* think about it," Drooler said. "Why would the witches stop there? You know how evil and covetous they are. Once they have Gravehome, soon they'll get bored and want something else. They'll give the Spirit of the Taiga more presents. Eventually, they're going to want *this very temple*."

For a long time, the Skeleton King was silent. He stroked his beard in quiet contemplation. What the zombie was saying seemed unlikely, and the easiest thing for the zombie king to do would be to ignore it. But a tiny seed of doubt began to grow in his hollow head. If what Drooler claimed came true, the Skeleton King would be in a very bad place, indeed. One that there might not be any escape from.

"This *is* most upsetting to hear, Drooler," the king eventually said. "Tell me, did you also come here with a plan for *solving* this problem? I could send my entire army to defend Gravehome, but I'm not sure that would work. As you say, the Spirit of the Taiga is enormous and very powerful. His fur looks so thick that it would absorb skeleton arrows. And his jaws are so big that he can eat a skeleton in a single bite."

"mmmm*Here's* where you're going to hate me even more," said Drooler. "I think that maybe the only thing that can save us is . . . the Bonesword."

"What?" said the Skeleton King. "The Bonesword is a ceremonial item, not an actual weapon. How could it help us?"

"mmmm*There* are several old zombie prophecies surrounding the Bonesword. One of them is that it will protect the zombies in our greatest hour of need. I think this might be it."

The Skeleton King stroked his beard and thought some more. Sometimes there were situations with no good solutions . . . only ones that were less bad than others. He was starting to think this might be one of those situations. If he'd had a proper chest, instead of just an empty ribcage, he would have felt a sinking feeling in it.

"This assault on Gravehome," the king asked. "Has it already begun?"

"mmmm*No*, I don't think so," answered Drooler. "But I think it will begin very soon. I hoped maybe the skeletons could help. Maybe by helping me find the Bonesword? I gave it to some witches to hide, and I don't know what they did with it."

"Lucky for you, I *do*," said the Skeleton King.

Drooler opened his mouth to ask how the king knew, but he could tell from his bony expression that the king's thoughts had suddenly drifted far away.

Specifically, they had drifted to the Fortress of Confusion, and the progress of Bacca and Dug. With a greater intensity than ever before, the Skeleton King hoped that they would find their way through the fortress, save the Bonesword, and return it as quickly as possible. The alternative was growing more and more unattractive with each passing moment.

In the meantime, the Skeleton King knew that he would have to act.

"Drooler, I will muster my armies and ride out to defend Gravehome," the Skeleton King said. "I do not know if we can defeat the Spirit of the Taiga, but we can at least buy Bacca and Dug some time. The rest, it appears, is going to be up to them."

CHAPTER FIFTEEN

eep within the Fortress of Confusion, Dug and Bacca crept slowly down the darkened corridor toward the new room ahead of them.

"mmmm*What* do you think's going to be in *this* one?" Dug asked excitedly. "Something else to build? Maybe another play to put on?"

"I dunno," said Bacca. "I'll bet it's definitely something we don't expect."

As if to confirm this speculation, they arrived at the doorway and peered inside to see . . . nothing at all.

It was a totally empty room, with a floor of brown and red sandstone blocks. The ceiling was high, and also sandstone. Sconces holding flaming torches were set into the walls. Across the room, on the opposite wall, was another closed door. It was covered in dust and also appeared magically sealed.

"mmmm*Do* you think we're getting close to the Bonesword?" Dug asked as they took a few careful steps inside.

"No, I expect we still have a ways to g—"

Bacca was not able to complete the thought. This was because he had tripped, which was weird because it was a completely empty room and there was nothing for him to trip over. Bacca reached forward with one hand to break his fall, expecting to topple over on the floor. Instead, as he leaned forward, his hand hit something solid. Something—something that felt suspiciously like a block—prevented him from falling completely over. What was even stranger was that there was nothing in front of him! The room was empty! And yet he stood there, leaning against what looked like air!

Dug had a similar encounter with an unseen barrier at the very same moment. Not being as agile as Bacca, Dug fell backward and landed in a heap on the sandstone floor.

"mmmm*Ouch*," Dug said.

"Are you okay?" asked Bacca, helping the young crafter to his feet.

"mmmm*I* think so," replied Dug. "But what in the Overworld is going on here? What did I just run into? There's nothing in this room!"

"Correction," said Bacca. "There's nothing *visible* in this room."

"mmmm*Are* you saying that there are invisible blocks in here?" Dug responded in astonishment. "Oh my goodness! I've never heard of such a thing."

"Just because you haven't heard of it, doesn't mean it doesn't exist," Bacca reminded him. "There's all kind of crazy stuff in the Overworld. Crazy, unimaginable, fantastic stuff! I wouldn't have believed half of it . . . if I hadn't seen it with my own eyes. Or, in this case, felt it with my own paws."

Bacca and Dug began to explore the room with their hands. However impossible it seemed, they quickly agreed that it was true: the room was full of blocks which were *completely invisible*. Bacca ran his paws from block to block, trying to imagine what bigger structure the blocks were a part of. They were not in orderly rows, but spread out all over the floor.

"Be careful," Bacca said as they explored. "I don't know if there will be traps, but something is definitely not right here. Stay cautious."

Dug felt his way forward, carefully moving to the side each time he encountered an invisible barrier in his path. Following Bacca's advice, he kept an eye out for anything that looked dangerous—but nothing did. At least as far as he could tell. Dug didn't really know how to tell if something invisible might be dangerous. He and Bacca were both making this up as they went along.

The blocks seemed to end near the far side of the room. Dug left them behind and kept advancing until he stood in front of the sealed door on the far side. Then he turned back to Bacca, who was carefully rapping on the side of an invisible block with his paw.

"mmmm*I* made it through!" Dug announced proudly.

"Good work . . . but I don't think it's a maze," replied Bacca, continuing to knock on the unseen block. "Otherwise, the door probably would have opened."

Dug thought about this for a moment. The door beside him stayed shut. Dug decided Bacca was probably right.

"This is totally strange," Bacca concluded, giving the invisible block a final blow with his fist. "I've heard of server planes where they have something called invisible bedrock, and other planes where crafters can use special tricks to make perfectly square, perfectly smooth invisible blocks called barriers, which can't be moved. But that's not what's happening here."

"mmmm*How* can you tell?" asked Dug.

"I'll show you," Bacca said.

As Dug watched, Bacca bent over and picked up an invisible block. It must have been very light, because Bacca only needed two fingers. Suddenly, Bacca cocked his arm like a baseball pitcher ready to throw a strike.

"Here you go," Bacca said. "Catch!"

Though nothing appeared to be in his hand, Bacca made a powerful throwing motion. Right at Dug's face.

Dug squinted his eyes and held up his hands to protect himself. Moments later something hit him. Something soft and fuzzy. It bounced off Dug's nose and came to rest a few feet away.

Dug opened his eyes. What had just happened? Whatever it was, it was totally strange. Bacca saw Dug's astonishment and broke into a fang-y grin. Dug felt his way around the floor until he found the invisible block. He picked it up and turned it over in his hands.

"mmmm*Wool!*" Dug exclaimed. "It's just a regular block of wool. Except invisible."

"Exactly," said Bacca. "These aren't perfectly smooth and immovable, so they're not barrier blocks. And they're not invisible bedrock because . . . well, they're not bedrock. At least not all of them. If you feel the blocks carefully with your hands, you'll realize that there are actually several different kinds."

Dug began to run his hands over the invisible blocks around him.

"mmmm*That's* crazy," he said. "You're right. They're all different."

"Some of the blocks will be easy to identify, even if we can't see them," Bacca said. "Wool, for example, is pretty much a no brainer. But others will be harder to nail down, even for an expert crafter like me. For example, andesite and diorite feel almost completely alike."

"mmmm*Is* identifying all the invisible blocks the trick to opening the door?" asked Dug.

"I'm not sure yet," Bacca replied. "These tests have all been pretty weird. They've also been pretty complicated. I'd be inclined to imagine it might be a little more involved—and a little stranger—than just identifying blocks. Let's have another look at the Tablet of Mystery."

"mmmm*Good* idea," agreed Dug. "It's funny . . . that Skeleton King told us the scratchy writing and pictures on this tablet were stuff that he and the other skeletons could never figure out. But we've figured them out *every time*. The king seems like a smart guy. I wonder why he was so confused by it."

"Remember, Dug, crafters are special," Bacca said, taking out the tablet. "We see the Overworld differently than others do. We know things that kings and queens don't know, and we can do things that kings and queens can't. A true crafter can look at a creation and instantly know why it looks the way it does. He or she understands how different structures can make people feel, because we craft feelings like a magician crafts tricks. Do you understand what I'm saying?"

Dug nodded. He did.

"Also," Bacca added with a smile, "that Skeleton King is a nice guy, but we might be just a *tiny* bit smarter than him. Don't tell him I said that."

Dug swore he wouldn't, but secretly he was very pleased.

As they had done twice before, Bacca and Dug began examining every inch of the Tablet of Mystery for clues. Both crafters remained silent for a time.

"mmmm*If* you were an ancient skeleton trying to draw a room full of invisible blocks, what would you draw?" Dug eventually asked. "A picture of nothing?"

"That would certainly be easy for the artist," Bacca quipped. "But I expect what we're looking for will be a little more complicated. Look for something involving different blocks. At least one of them will be wool."

Dug and Bacca scoured the Tablet of Mystery some more. There were so many markings, and most made no sense in this context. Others looked as though they had been made by accident, possibly by all the skeletons who had handled the tablet in the thousands of years since its creation. In a few places around the edges, bits had even been chipped away. Both crafters secretly worried that an important piece could be missing.

After several more minutes of silent study, Dug said, "mmmm*Look* at this little guy."

His dried-up zombie finger pointed to a spot in the center of the tablet where a stick figure stood inside a box. He looked just like an average stick figure, with one exception. His legs and arms were angled forward, like he was gesturing with both his hands and feet.

"What about him?" Bacca asked. "He's sort of pointing, isn't he? Do you think—what?—that he's pointing at invisible blocks?"

Dug shook his head no.

"mmmm*Maybe* he's not pointing," Dug said. "Maybe his arms and legs are like that because that's how he stands. Because he's a sheep."

Bacca and Dug both looked over at the space nearby where the invisible block of wool rested silently.

"And sheep are made of wool," Bacca said. "I mean . . . basically, they are. There's some meat and stuff, but a lot of it is wool."

Bacca and Dug agreed that this was an interesting lead. They decided to investigate further. If the stick figure was a sheep, then what was the thing surrounding it?

"mmmm*It's* like a box. Or a rectangle. It's longer than it is tall, but that doesn't give me much to go on."

"Are the sheep's feet touching the floor of the box?" Bacca asked.

Dug looked closely.

"mmmm*No*," Dug said. "Raised a little bit. Like it's floating."

"Or standing on something," Bacca said.

Dug looked up from the Tablet of Mystery and stared at Bacca. The zombie's expression made it clear that he didn't understand.

"Maybe we're going about this in the wrong order," Bacca said, drumming his claws. "Maybe instead of starting with the tablet . . . we need to start with the blocks."

"mmmm*How*?" asked Dug. "I thought we already did that."

"Maybe we have to build a structure with a sheep inside it," said Bacca. "We don't know what kind of structure, but different kinds of structures are made from different kinds of crafting materials. So let's figure out the crafting material we have, and then figure out what kind of structure it could build. We'll work backwards."

"mmmm*Okay*," Dug said. "It will be hard to figure out what some of these blocks are when we can't see them. Like you said, they're not all as squishy as wool."

"Don't worry," Bacca replied. "I've got some ideas for how we can do it."

They started by gathering all the invisible blocks together in a pile. To do this, Bacca and Dug began walking carefully across the seemingly empty room, standing side-by side. They covered every inch of floor, like they were mowing a lawn. Whenever they hit an invisible block, they moved it to a designated spot beside the magically sealed door. They encountered several different kinds of blocks as they did this. Some were heavy and some were light. Some were smooth and some were rough.

"Don't worry about figuring out what they are right now," Bacca said as Dug held an invisible block near his ear and shook it. "We'll do that when we've got them collected."

Soon, the entire room was cleared. All the blocks were in an invisible pile.

"mmmm*Whew*," said Dug. "That was a lot of work."

"If you want to be a good crafter, you have to learn to like working hard," Bacca said. "We're just getting started. Next, we're going to sort the blocks into three categories: hard, soft, and something else."

"mmmm*Okay*," said Dug. "But what's 'something else'?"

"You'll know it when you feel it," Bacca told him with a grin.

The two crafters began grouping the blocks by the way they felt—hard with hard, and soft with soft. Most were indeed hard, but a few were soft and squishy. Others—as Bacca had predicted—were hard to classify.

"mmmm*I'm* putting this in the 'something else' pile," Dug said, holding up an invisible block. "It's hard but not solid. I can put my hand through parts of it. See?"

"Good," said Bacca. "We'll go back to it later."

"mmmm*This* one also goes in the same pile," Dug said, holding up another. "It's pointy."

"Put it on the pile," Bacca said, and Dug did.

When they were finished sorting, Bacca saw—or rather *felt*—that they had many hard blocks of crafting material, a few blocks in the 'something else' category, and just a handful that were soft.

"Good, good," Bacca said, standing with his arms crossed proudly. "We're making progress. Now let's go category by category, and try to classify them further. I'm hoping that we don't have to guess all of them correctly, only enough to get a general idea of the structure we have to build."

"mmmm*Can* we start with the soft blocks?" Dug asked. "There are the fewest number of them."

"Good thinking," said Bacca.

Dug approached the invisible pile of soft blocks, and began to carefully investigate them with his rotting hands.

"mmmm*Five* blocks total in this category," Dug said, setting them before Bacca.

"Three are clearly wool," Bacca said, giving each a squeeze. "These other two are some kind of meat. I'm going to go ahead and guess mutton."

"mmmm*How* can you be sure?" Dug asked.

"Take a taste if you like," Bacca said. "Me, I prefer raw fish. Pretty much exclusively."

"mmmm*I* only eat people," Dug said.

"Touché. So we'll just have to trust my instincts," Bacca said. "And I think we're supposed to build a sheep out of it. Maybe like a statue."

"mmmm*I've* never made a sheep before," said Dug. "That will be a fun change of pace."

Bacca moved down the line to the pile of invisible blocks that fell into the "something else" category. It was the second-largest pile.

"Okay," Bacca said. "Let's see what we have here."

Bacca picked up the nearest invisible block from this category. It was lighter than a block of stone or rock, but heavier than wool or mutton. Parts of it were solid, but other parts he could run his paw right through. He tapped on it with his claws, trying to get a feel for the material.

"This has slats on it, and it's made from wood," Bacca concluded. "Wood sticks, in particular."

"mmmm*Slats* with wood . . . hmm," Dug said. "So maybe a rail for a minecar?"

"Rails have some wood, but they're mostly iron," Bacca said, shaking his head. "This is entirely wood. One, two, three . . . feels like seven wood sticks total."

"mmmm*A* ladder is seven wooden sticks!" Dug said.

"Right!" said Bacca. "So that's got to be what it is."

Bacca set the invisible ladder to the side. Then, on the sandstone floor in front of it, he scratched the word "Ladder" so he would remember what it was.

"Okay," Bacca said. "You do the next one, Dug."

Dug crept to the pile of invisible blocks and felt around until he found one. He picked it up and turned it over and over. He felt it with his hands and scratched it with his long zombie fingernails. He held it up to his rotting ear and gave it a knock with his knuckle.

"mmmm*This* is very similar to a ladder . . . but it's *not* a ladder," Dug concluded. "It's still got slats though."

To illustrate this, Dug passed his arm through parts of the block.

"Okay," said Bacca. "Keep going."

"mmmm*There's* no metal in it," Dug said. "It's more than just sticks, though. It's got wood planks that I can distinctly feel. Four of them. The wood smells like . . . cedar, I think."

"Very good," said Bacca. "So what has no metal, sticks, and four cedar planks? And feels like a ladder, but isn't a ladder?"

"mmmm*A* fence!" said Dug proudly. "This block is part of a fence!"

"You know, I think you're right," said Bacca.

They put the block on the ground and etched the word "Fence" beside it. To stay organized, Bacca suggested they continue going through the "something else" pile until they had extracted all of the other pieces of ladder and fence. They felt their way around the invisible blocks and found several more sections of both. Then Dug piped up.

"mmmm*This* one is strange," Dug said, holding up a new block that appeared heavy. "It's got slats like a ladder or a rail, but it's neither of those. It's metal. Iron."

"It's iron bars then," said Bacca. "People use them a lot like fences. Sometime they use them to make arrow slits on castles. Hmmm. We *are* learning things, aren't we? Our sheep is surrounded by something with ladders, fences, and arrows slits. I wonder what it could be. Let's keep working!"

Bacca and Dug kept looking through the pile. They found three torches, which were easy enough to identify on account of being long and thin and having one end that was too hot to touch for long, an invisible chest which could be identified *via* the padlock on the front, and a strange wooden block that seemed to have slats at the top, but not at the bottom.

"mmmm*What* kind of block has openings at the top, but not the bottom?" Dug wondered.

"Trying running your hands around the edges," Bacca suggested.

Dug obediently felt along the edges of the block.

"mmmm*There* are hinges," Dug said. "Two metal hinges. Like for a cabinet or a cupboard or a . . . door!"

"Now you've got it," Bacca said. "This is the door to the . . . to the . . . whatever *this* is."

Dug and Bacca felt around the rest of the pile where they had stacked the 'something else' blocks.

"I don't feel any more," Bacca said. "That must be all of them. We're going to have to move on to the final group—the heavy blocks. I think this is going to be the most challenging. It's going to take all of our skill and cleverness to determine what these blocks are made of."

"mmmm*Let's* do it!" said Dug, practically diving into the invisible pile of blocks. Bacca was pleased to see this sort of enthusiasm (and also pleased that Dug had had the sense not to *actually* dive into a pile of hard blocks).

They began picking up the heavy crafting materials and inspecting their surfaces.

"Look for ways in which the blocks are different from one another," said Bacca. "Any difference is important, even small ones. Don't underestimate tiny details."

After a minute, Dug brought an invisible block over to Bacca.

"mmmm*This* one has moss on it," Dug said, handing it to Bacca. "See? You can feel it."

"That's definitely an important detail," Bacca said. "Good work."

"mmmm*It's* probably moss stone, right?" said Dug. "Almost all stone with moss growing on it is moss stone. So isn't that what we should assume? It's like that old saying that zombie doctors have: 'If you hear approaching feet, it's probably a zombie and *not* a zombie pigman.'"

"Normally, I'd say yes," replied Bacca. "But run your hands over it again. What do you feel *underneath* the moss?"

Had he missed something? Dug took the invisible block back from Bacca and carefully felt along each side.

"mmmm*There* are long straight grooves underneath the moss," Dug said. "And other grooves running across those. Almost like it's . . . "

"Made of bricks," Bacca said, finishing the thought.

Dug's jaw dropped. Not quite off his face, but still lower than it would drop on a normal person.

"mmmm*Mossy* stone bricks!" Dug said when he had recovered. "That's what this is. It's slightly different from moss stone."

"A slight difference, but an important one," Bacca said. "Mossy stone bricks are only found in a few places. I think you just narrowed down our options for what this might be."

"mmmm*I* did?" said Dug. "I mean . . . yeah, I guess I did!"

Bacca and Dug made a stack of the invisible mossy stone bricks and marked it, then turned their attention to the remaining blocks. They found several that also had the grooves running across them, and more that had grooves but also other, tinier lines.

"Stone bricks and cracked stone bricks," Bacca pronounced.

"mmmm*Is* that important?" Dug asked.

"It does narrow things down even more," Bacca said confidently. "Based on this, I'm feeling pretty sure that the remaining invisible blocks are going to include some arrangement of cobblestone, stone brick stairs, and stone brick slabs. Why don't you go ahead and see if I'm right?"

Dug obediently rummaged through the pile of remaining invisible blocks and tried to feel the differences between them. As he did so, his eyes began to widen.

"mmmm*You're* exactly right!" Dug said. "How did you know?"

"Think about it," Bacca said, taking a seat on an invisible block. "Very few structures have mossy stone bricks. So think about what has *those* blocks, plus iron bars, fences, torches, and all the other stuff we've already found . . ."

Dug thought. As a young zombie, his experience of the Overworld was far smaller than Bacca's. His zombie parents never let him stray far from home. It was for his own good, they said. (They claimed they were just trying to keep him out of the sunlight, but Dug had his doubts.) Therefore, most of Dug's exposure to the Overworld had come not from exploring firsthand, but from crafting.

Dug understood that crafting materials didn't exist in a vacuum. They were all connected. They were connected to each other, as well as the rest of the Overworld. Because of this, Dug had been able to learn a surprising amount about the Overworld. In fact, Dug knew the Overworld better than many world travelers, even though his voyage with Bacca was his first real trip across it.

"mmmm*It's* got to be a stronghold," Dug said after a long and deep consideration. "They have mossy stone bricks, and also all of the other blocks we've found. Strongholds are very, very rare. They occur underground, and have absolutely everything we've found here . . . except for a sheep."

"I think you're right," Bacca said.

"mmmm*So* should we get to work?" Dug asked, lifting an invisible block.

"I'm ready if you are," Bacca said. "Let's make a nice stronghold for our little sheep."

Bacca and Dug began crafting. Right away, Dug saw the wisdom of organizing the invisible blocks and writing down which were which. It made construction go much more quickly. Bacca and Dug began by putting down a floor, and then made walls out of the different kinds of stone bricks. Then

they created a central platform in the middle of the
stronghold, with stone brick stairs leading up to it.

"Here is where we should place the sheep,"
Bacca said. "Do you want to do the honors?"

Dug held up the mutton and wool, unsure of
how to begin.

"mmmm*Neither* of my parents are crafters," Dug
said. "But my father used to tell a scary story about
a crafter who lived many years ago in a faraway
land. His name was Franken-something. He used
parts like this to craft things that were alive!"

"Yeah, I've heard of that guy," Bacca replied.
"I've also heard things didn't turn out so well for
him. I don't think we need to make a *real* sheep.
That would probably end up badly for *us* too. Why
don't you just use this crafting material to make
something that *looks* like a sheep?"

"mmmm*Whew*," said Dug. "Okay. That sounds
safer."

While Dug worked on the sheep, Bacca placed
torches on the walls of the room—even though they
were invisible and seemed to cast no light—and
ladders on the sides of the raised platform. Bacca
had seen many strongholds before. He had a good
idea of how to craft one so that it looked right.
But easier said then done when all the blocks you
were using were invisible! It was useless to take a
step back from his work and see how it all looked,
because there was nothing to see. (This also frustrated Bacca, because it gave you very little sense
of accomplishment, even when you were nearly finished with your creation, and that was one of the
best things about being a crafter.)

As Dug assembled the sheep atop the platform,
it looked like Dug was magically hovering several

feet in the air. That was a weird thing to watch! But, after the better part of an hour, everything seemed to be in place. Every few moments, Dug closed his eyes and felt the contours of the sheep he had created.

"mmmm*Lots* of zombies don't have eyes," Dug said. "Often they lose them in accidents or they just rot out of their heads. I wish we had one of those zombies with us now. They have great senses of touch. They would definitely know the feel of a sheep. I'm not sure this sheep is very good at all. The eyes and snout are too big, and the wool's kind of lopsided."

"I wouldn't worry," Bacca said. "It doesn't need to win a sheep beauty contest. It just has to look a little like a sheep."

"mmmm*That's* good," said Dug. "Because I think this is the best I can do."

Appearing to walk on air, Dug descended from the raised platform down the stone brick stairs until he stood beside Bacca.

Dug was about to ask what would happen next, but before he could speak a strange mist began to fill the room around them.

"mmmm*What* is this?" Dug wondered out loud. "Omigosh! What's happening?"

Bacca smiled from ear to ear.

"I think we did it!" Bacca said excitedly.

As they watched, the mist grew thicker and began to spread. Soon, it was hard to see anything at all. Then, just as suddenly as it had arrived, the mist began to clear. When it did, it revealed a perfectly-crafted stronghold, exactly like the ones Bacca had encountered out in the wild. The only difference was that this one had a sheep inside of it. A real one, apparently. As Bacca and Dug looked on in surprise, the sheep on top of the platform opened its eyes. And then its mouth.

"Baaaa," it said.

"mmmm*Oh* my goodness!" said Dug. "I made a real sheep. I'm like that Franken-person. Oh no!"

Bacca saw it another way.

"I don't think we did that . . . I think *the fortress* made our sheep come alive," Bacca said as they watched the animal slowly descend the staircase leading down from the platform. "Keep in mind, this *is* a magical place."

"mmmm*Oh*," said Dug. "Still, I hope he doesn't blame me for his wool being crooked."

The sheep walked over to the magically sealed door. After a few moments, there was a grating sound and the door began to open.

The sheep glanced over at Bacca and Dug as if to say: "Well, are you coming?" Then it walked through the opening.

"Should we see what waits in the next room?" Bacca asked.

"mmmm*I* guess so," said Dug. It was clear that Dug was still a little stunned at the sight of the sheep he had crafted actually walking around.

Bacca took the astonished zombie reassuringly by the shoulder and led him through the door and into the tunnel beyond.

CHAPTER SIXTEEN

The tunnel led down into the heart of the fortress. The walls were lit with more ancient glowstones. They cast an eerie light that never flickered or changed. The sheep walked several paces ahead of Bacca and Dug. The animal seemed confident, like it knew where it was going.

"mmmm*This* tunnel is kind of scary," Dug said.

"Hey, you're at least as brave as a sheep, right?" Bacca said. "And he's not afraid."

"mmmm*I* guess so," agreed Dug.

They followed the sheep.

After journeying down, down, down—to a point that Bacca surmised must be deep beneath the fortress's cliff face—they reached an open doorway. The sheep passed through it and walked out of sight.

Bacca and Dug approached cautiously and peered into the room beyond. It was a cavernous place with a very high ceiling. The corners of the room were crowded with crafting materials that were very old and covered in dust. It gave Bacca the feeling of discovering a long-abandoned construction site. There was a door on the other side of the room, and it was the grandest-looking door they'd seen so far, encrusted with diamond and emerald blocks that shined as if newly-polished. It was also—quite astonishingly—forty feet above the ground. Just to reach it, Bacca reckoned he would have to build a long ladder. But that was not even the strangest part of this room.

In the middle of the cavernous floor was a ramp. It led up to the jeweled door . . . or rather, it once had. The ramp was supported by two pillars, but there had clearly once been a middle pillar that had long ago been destroyed or removed. Only an empty base remained. Consequently, with nothing to support its center, the middle of the ramp had fallen to the floor. Another interesting detail was that the two remaining pillars—each easily thirty feet high—had been carved into statues. The first pillar, the one farthest from the door, had been crafted to resemble a villager. The third pillar, closest to the door, portrayed a skeleton—bow in hand. There was no clue as to what the missing, middle pillar might have been.

"mmmm*Huh*," Dug said, surveying this strange sight. "At least it's clear where we're supposed to go. That sparkly door doesn't leave much mystery. The challenge is going to be getting up to it!"

Bacca agreed. Both crafters turned their attention to the ruined ramp. Made of wood planks, it had splintered and split when the middle support column had been removed.

"mmmm*Zombies* aren't very good jumpers," Dug said. "But you're a great jumper, Bacca. Wash down a Potion of Leaping or two, and I'm positive you'll be able to clear that part where the ramp is broken."

"Yeah," Bacca said, still carefully surveying the strange room. "I'm sure I could. The problem is, I don't know if *he* could."

"mmmm*Huh?*" Dug said, puzzled. "What do you mean by—"

"Baaaa."

Dug was cut off by the loud bleating of the sheep. The creature stood at the foot of the ramp. It looked over at Bacca and Dug, then up at the door.

"I think we need to get that sheep up to that door along with us," Bacca said. "The sheep can't jump. It has to walk up the ramp."

Dug nodded in agreement. Based on how the fortress had behaved previously, he knew his teacher was likely right.

"On the other hand, building a new support column and fixing a ramp should be pretty easy to do," Bacca continued. "The only question is . . . what's it supposed to look like?"

"mmmm*Look* like?" said Dug.

"Yeah," said Bacca. "One's a villager, and the other's a skeleton. So what's supposed to stand between them? This room is full of all sorts of materials that we could use for crafting. I think that might be part of the challenge. There are a lot of different things we could make. It's up to us to figure out which is the right one."

Dug surveyed the crafting materials piled around the edges of the room. They could use this stuff to make almost anything. The possibilities were almost paralyzingly limitless.

"mmmm*Let's* look at the—"

"Way ahead of you," Bacca said, taking the Tablet of Mystery out of his inventory.

It was then that disaster struck.

The blocks of wool that Bacca and Dug had used to build the sheep were very oily. But neither had quite realized how much of the oil had rubbed off on their hands (and paws). As Bacca gestured for Dug to grip the other half of the tablet—so that they could both hold it together—he felt the heavy, ancient prismarine beginning to slip from his grasp.

"Ack!" Bacca shouted. "Dug! Help!"

Unfortunately, Dug's hands were even slicker than Bacca's. Dug had spent much more time handling the wool. The tablet went right through Dug's hands like warm butter. There was a desperate moment where the two crafters bobbled the heavy tablet back and forth, and then a horrible "BOOM!" as the prismarine fell crashing to the cavern floor.

It splintered into a thousand tiny pieces.

Bacca and Dug looked down at the ruined Tablet of Mystery, then up at one another.

"mmmm*Oh* gosh!" cried Dug. "The tablet! I didn't know our hands were so greasy! How are we ever going to figure out what to do?"

Dug looked as though he might cry. Bacca, in contrast, put a comforting hand on Dug's shoulder and even managed a smile.

"Eh, could be worse," Bacca pronounced. "But I don't think the Skeleton King is going to be very happy when he finds out about this. Do you mind being the one to tell him?"

"mmmm*Maybe* we could piece it back together," Dug said hopefully.

"Yeah . . . if we had about a month to work on it," Bacca quipped. "And we definitely don't. The thing was so old, it just completely shattered. Face it, Dug. It's gone."

"mmmm*Then* what are we—" Dug began.

"We're going to figure it out on our own," Bacca said confidently. "*That's* what we're going to do. Sometimes part of being a crafter is improvisation.

Things don't always go as you plan. But when disaster strikes, you're not allowed to give up. You have to pick yourself up, dust yourself off, and find a way to keep going. You have to use the resources around you to figure out a new solution. Frankly, that might be the *most* important part of being a crafter."

"mmmm*Oh*," said Dug. "OK. Sorry for being pessimistic."

"That's okay," Bacca said. "It happens to everybody sometimes. Now we just need to put on our thinking caps and figure out how to solve this problem without the tablet. The training wheels are off, kid. This is the real test."

"Baaaa."

Bacca and Dug looked over to the bottom of the ramp. The sheep stopped one of its hooves, clearly getting impatient.

"Hang on," Bacca said to it. "We're trying our best over here."

Dug walked over to the piles of crafting materials stacked along the edges of the room. He began rifling through them. Bacca joined him. You could make almost *anything* with the crafting materials here, Bacca thought, but the blocks themselves weren't going to provide a hint in any particular direction or another.

Then Bacca noticed that Dug had stopped searching. The zombie rested his fist against his chin and appeared very deep in thought.

"Got something?" Bacca asked.

"mmmm*Maybe,*" Dug said. "It's just an idea. I want to see if they have prismarine here."

"They do," Bacca said. "There's a bunch over here by me. You're not thinking of trying to rebuild the Tablet of Mystery or something?"

"mmmm*No*," Dug said. "Nothing like that. Now where was the prismarine again?"

Bacca pointed the way. Dug hurried over and found an abundance of it. There was prismarine, prismarine bricks, and dark prismarine. An enormous amount. Enough to craft something really, really large.

"mmmm*Okay* then . . . I think maybe I know what we have to build," Dug said.

"What?" Bacca asked. "How did you figure it out?"

"mmmm*Well* . . . I . . . uh . . . "

For the first time that he could recall, Dug seemed embarrassed to tell Bacca what he wanted to craft.

"It's okay," Bacca said. "You can tell me."

Dug still chose not to answer directly.

"mmmm*Do* you ever feel like you *might* know what you want to craft . . . but you're certain that it'll either be awesome and everybody will love it . . . or else it'll be totally wrong and people will make fun of you for trying something so stupid?"

"Sure," Bacca said. "All the time. But if you don't make a point to challenge yourself and try those projects that seem weird or scary—or that you know might not work—then you lose out on some of the most important breakthroughs that help you move to the next level as a crafter!"

Bacca was secretly pleased that Dug had told him this, because he knew this was the kind of thing the young zombie needed to think about in order to reach a new stage with his crafting. Bacca and LadyBacc had already showed Dug all they could teach him. From here on out, he was going to have to learn by trial and error. That would take courage, and courage wasn't something that anybody could teach. It had to come from within Dug himself.

"mmmm*Okay*," said Dug. "That makes me feel better . . . but I'm still nervous to tell you what it is."

"How about this," Bacca said. "*Don't* tell me what it is. Just craft it. Then we'll see if it works."

"Baaaa."

"We are *working on it*," Bacca grumbled to the impatient sheep.

Feeling inspired by Bacca's words, Dug began hauling blocks of prismarine over to the spot where a new pillar needed to be built.

As pleased as Bacca was to see Dug taking this initiative, he was also secretly relieved. Bacca had no guess yet about what the central column needed to be.

As Bacca watched, Dug began to carve two enormous legs. Bacca had had his own experience crafting very large statues. Once while solving a series of riddles, he crafted statues of three enormous villagers—so that an equally enormous skeleton could shoot arrows at them. That had been a fun one.

Bacca watched Dug's statue grow before his eyes, and thought it looked very good. The only weak point was the color scheme. He was working with far too many greens and blues. It made it look like the subject was under water. As Dug got up to the arms and the torso, he switched to an even deeper shade of green using the dark prismarine. Now it looked as though the statue had stuck its arms down into some yucky green swamp, and they'd come out covered in muck.

Then, suddenly, Bacca realized what Dug was doing.

Like looking at an optical illusion for long enough, the answer suddenly clicked in Bacca's brain.

The furry crafter smiled to himself. Now Dug's approach made total sense. The only question remaining was: was it a self-portrait?

Dug was crafting a huge, thirty-foot zombie. He'd used different kinds of prismarine to get all the shades of decaying zombie flesh absolutely right. He'd used polished diorite and polished andesite to make the zombie's grey shoes. Now he was using blocks of coal to make the zombie's tiny, black eyes. As Dug put on the finishing touches, Bacca decided that it *wasn't* supposed to be a portrait of the crafter. It was an entirely new zombie. Dug's shoulders weren't quite as wide as this zombie's, and Dug's neck was a little thinner.

After he finished topping off the statue's head with a flat block of prismarine, Dug hopped back down to the floor and started gathering the shattered pieces of wood from the broken ramp. Crafting them together, Dug began to reconstruct the ramp section by section, using the top of the zombie head as one of the supports.

The sheep watched Dug work. Bacca, in turn, watched the sheep and made a 'be patient' motion with his paws. Finally, the ramp was finished. Dug strode across it several times, testing it. The finished product seemed to be strong and study. Pleased with his work, Dug climbed back down to the bottom of the ramp.

"mmmm*There* you go, little guy," Dug said to the sheep. "I hope this was what you wanted."

There was a tense moment while she sheep hesitated. It turned its head to the left and then to the right, appearing to carefully inspect the work that the young crafter had done. Then, momentously, the sheep lifted a tiny hoof and placed it on the ramp. Then another. And another still.

Soon, the wooly beast was making its way carefully up the ramp. It crossed the statue of the villager, the zombie, and then the skeleton, before finally arriving at the jeweled door. The sheep then let out a satisfied, "Baaaa."

A familiar rumbling sound began, and the jeweled door began to open by itself. Slowly and confidently, the sheep passed through. Whatever room might be found beyond the open doorway was not clear, but strange reflections shone out from it, like golden light reflecting off the surface of water.

"mmmm*Wow!*" Dug said. "I was right! It worked."

The young zombie began to head up the ramp, following the sheep.

"Wait a second," said Bacca. "How did you know to do that, Dug? I'm really impressed."

"mmmm*I* just had a weird idea and went with it," Dug said.

"Tell me about this 'weird idea,'" Bacca insisted.

"mmmm*Well*, I started thinking about how skeletons come from villagers," Dug said. "So then I also started thinking about how zombies come from villagers too. I mean, with zombies it's much faster. A zombie can turn a villager into another zombie pretty much instantly, by biting it. With skeletons, it takes a whole lot longer. Skeletons spawn when there's a bunch of bones just left somewhere. Eventually, those bones animate, grab a bow, and start shooting people—and boom, you've got a skeleton. But the idea I had was that *both* skeletons and zombies begin as villagers."

"I see," said Bacca.

"mmmm*Then* I started thinking about how you could start as a villager, then get bitten and become a zombie, but then maybe a crafter whacks you with a weapon and you fall back down and just start decomposing. And maybe when you decompose enough until you're just bones, then you get to come back *again* . . . as a skeleton."

Bacca was quiet. He had never thought about this before, but it felt as though the little zombie's idea could be quite important. He was intrigued, to say the least.

"You may just be on to something, Dug," Bacca said. "I know that skeletons have no memory of who they were in life. Is the same true for zombies?"

Dug nodded his head.

"mmmm*Yes*. We don't know who we were before we were reanimated or infected. It's always a big mystery."

"Just as I thought," said Bacca. "And we've always assumed that skeletons had no memory of being villagers. So then maybe they had no memory . . . of being zombies."

"mmmm*I* sure am learning a lot on this trip!" Dug said brightly.

"Yeah," said Bacca, feeling a little astonished. "I am too."

Together they followed the sheep's path up the ramp and across the top of the cavernous room until they stood before the jeweled doorway. Bacca saw that beyond was a medium-sized room of andesite blocks. In the middle of the room was a pool of water. The water reflected natural light from above. This meant that the ceiling of the room might extend all the way to the top of the cliff. In

the center of the watery pool was a very fancy orna-
mental table made of sandstone. Displayed on the
table was what looked for all the Overworld like a
long sword crafted out of bone. The sheep stood at
the edge of the pool and smiled.

"mmmm*Oh my gosh!*" Dug stammered. "Is that
it? Have we found the Bonesword?"

Before Bacca could open his mouth to answer,
the sound of a single pair of footsteps echoed somewhere on the andesite floor.

Tic-tac. Tic-tac. Tic-tac.

Then the footsteps stopped. Again there was
silence. The sheep hadn't moved.

With the speed of an expert gunfighter, Bacca's
diamond axe was out of his inventory and ready in
his hand.

"Dug," Bacca whispered. "I don't think we're
alone."

CHAPTER SEVENTEEN

Bacca crept into the room with Betty raised high. His eyes scanned for the source of the footsteps—or for any movement at all—but he saw nothing. Moving deeper inside revealed strange architecture. The walls were decorated with large skulls crafted out of blocks of polished diorite. The skulls' mouths were open, and easily big enough for a person to fit inside. There was a door on the far wall, past the watery pool. However, it did not appear to be magical or locked. In fact—as he looked more closely—Bacca saw that it was slightly open. The walls of the room extended up hundreds of feet. The room had no ceiling, only metal grates at the roof to keep out the curious (and, Bacca supposed, birds).

There was one more striking feature to the room. Standing beside the slightly-open door were three skeletons perched on sandstone platforms. One was made from iron, another was made from gold, and the third seemed to have been crafted from actual bone. In each of their hands were swords crafted out of the very same materials.

Bacca carefully moved in a full circle around the room, scanning for any clues. For the moment, he ignored the bony sword in the center of the pond. It was still not obvious to him who or what had made the sound of footsteps. Bacca wanted to make sure he and Dug were completely safe before they turned their attention to the Bonesword.

Bacca heard Dug tentatively enter the room behind him.

"mmmm*What* if there's somebody in here . . . who is *invisible*?" Dug nervously whispered. "There were invisible blocks two rooms ago. Maybe now there are invisible *people*."

"Maybe," said Bacca, still circling the room carefully. He kept a close eye on the giant skeleton heads, and well as the three sculptures. Betty glistened in the light shining down from the openings in the roof.

Dug looked back and forth between the sculptures and the Bonesword in the center of the pool.

"mmmm*Is* this some kind of trick . . . or trap?" Dug asked.

Bacca smiled to himself. He knew that it almost certainly was. At the very least, a sixth sense told him things in this room were not as they seemed. Bacca was brave and clever, and part of him didn't mind this challenge. There was hardly any enemy he couldn't defeat. However, Bacca also reminded himself that he had a young crafter to protect. If only for this reason, he decided he must be careful in the moments ahead and not act hastily.

Bacca crept to the edge of the pool. He stuck his paw in, testing the water. It was cool and clear. It did not seem to be magical.

"mmmm*I* have the feeling that we're being watched," said Dug. "Do you have the same feeling?"

Bacca turned away from the pool and gave Dug a look that said 'Would you prefer to wait outside?'

"mmmm*I'm* just saying . . . " Dug said timidly. "It feels like something is watching us. And not just the sheep."

Bacca had the same feeling.

Rather than wading into the pool and grabbing the sword, Bacca walked to the slightly-open door on the far side of the room. It appeared to be a completely normal door. No decorations. Not magic. Nothing special. Bacca stuck his toe inside, and used his foot to push it the rest of the way open. There was a loud *creeeeeeeak* as the rusty hinges moved.

Beyond the door was a small but very pleasant room. It looked like living quarters. It had a fireplace, couches and chairs, a table, a bed, and a library filled with books. Bacca stepped inside and ran a hairy finger across the table. Not only was it free from dust, but it had been meticulously cleaned. Either somebody had lived here very recently, or somebody *still* lived here.

There was no other sign of life. Bacca thought again of Dug's idea of an invisible inhabitant. Investigating further, he walked to the bookcase and pulled out the nearest book. He could read it, but only with great difficulty. This was because it was written entirely in Ancient Skeleton.

Now Bacca had the clues he was looking for. He walked confidently back to where Dug was waiting beside the pool. The zombie glanced anxiously back at forth between the three armed skeletons, and then between the giant skulls on the walls.

Bacca ignored the pool, the large skeleton heads, and even the sheep. Instead, he turned to face the three life-size skeleton statues—one of iron, one of gold, and one of bone.

"Let's see . . . " Bacca said, addressing all three at once. "If you'd known we were coming, you might have had time to paint yourself with gold or iron. But we heard you shuffling into place right when we walked in, so I'm guessing we surprised you. You probably barely had time to grab the Bonesword . . . "

Bacca stepped forward and used Betty to prod the sword held by the skeleton made of bone. The reaction was instantaneous. The skeleton sprang to life and jumped backward off of his podium.

"Aha!" said Bacca. "I knew it."

The skeleton crossed its arms and looked sternly at Bacca. It did not seem intimidated.

"You must be the Skeleton King's brother," Bacca said. "He said to tell you, 'No hard feelings,' by the way."

"Who are you, and why have you come here?" asked the skeleton in a stern, bony voice.

"I'm Bacca, and this is my friend Dug," Bacca answered. "The Bonesword has been stolen and the zombies are at war with the skeletons because of it. We heard it was hidden here in this fortress, so we came to get it. We need you to give it back to us so we can stop the war. We're also in a bit of a bind, time-wise. There's a ceasefire, but it's going to run out soon, and then they'll start fighting again. So if you could be quick about it . . . that'd be great."

The skeleton kept his arms crossed.

"Tell me, have you actually *seen* the Bonesword before?" the skeleton asked skeptically.

"I'll know it when I see it," Bacca answered. "Sword made from half a femur. Engraved with important scenes from zombie history. Sharpened to a deadly point at one end. All of which describes the sword in your hand perfectly."

The skeleton nodded. He took a few steps toward Bacca, and held out the weapon. Bacca leaned in close and examined the blade.

"Yes," Bacca said. "That looks like what I just described."

"A bat came to drop it through a hole in the roof," explained the skeleton. "I reached up and grabbed it."

"That was the doing of some witches," Bacca explained. "They were part of the conspiracy to take the Bonesword. Don't worry about it. They're on my list. But anyhow, will you please give me the sword now?"

He didn't know how powerful this skeleton was, but Bacca was ready for a fight if need be. At the same time, like any wise crafter, Bacca always avoided unnecessary conflict. He would give the skeleton a chance to hand it over peacefully.

Which, to Bacca's amazement, was exactly what the skeleton did.

The skeleton brought the sword up to Bacca's chest and suddenly let it fall. His hands still slick from the wool, Bacca barely caught it before it hit the floor. Bacca scowled at the skeleton. *No need to be a jerk about it*, he thought.

From behind them, Dug spoke up.

"mmmm*I* have a question, Mr. Skeleton."

"Tibia," the skeleton said. "My name is Tibia."

"mmmm*I* have a question, Tibia," Dug said. "Why do you have that *other* sword in the middle of that pond? It's also made of bone. Is it a fake Bonesword? Some kind of trick, so that people come here and take the wrong one?"

The skeleton laughed.

"That," he said, pointing at the bony blade that rested on the sandstone display in the center of the pool, "is the Bonesword."

"Wait, then this . . . ?" Bacca said, holding up the blade in his hands.

" . . . is *also* the Bonesword," the skeleton added.

"mmmm*Uh-oh*," said Dug. "Now I'm confused. How can they *both* be the Bonesword? Is there more than one? The Zombie King didn't say anything about that."

Bacca looked over at the sword on the sandstone table. An idea struck him. As Dug and the skeleton watched, Bacca waded out into the pool and snatched the other sword. Then he waded back out and held both blades next to one another, comparing them.

"These are two swords carved from the same femur," Bacca said.

"Correct," said Tibia.

"But where one has carvings of ancient zombie history on it, this other one has engravings of . . . ancient skeletons!" Bacca said.

"mmmm*What*?" said Dug. "Let me see."

Bacca handed over the swords to his apprentice. Dug held them up to the light streaming down from the openings far above and carefully examined them. Bacca was right! The carvings running down the blade of this second sword were clearly of skeletons. And both swords had come from the same bone.

"mmmm*Two* Boneswords?" Dug asked. "What does this mean?"

"I've got some pretty good guesses," Bacca said, "but I'll bet our friend can tell us for certain."

They both looked at Tibia.

"Indeed, I can," said the skeleton. There was a hint of sadness in the skeleton's bony voice. He had no features to read, but his shoulders slumped as if he now recalled a great tragedy.

"The weapons you hold both date from ancient times," Tibia continued. "Thousands of years ago, there was a knowledge that today has been lost. But by solving the puzzle that took you into this room, you may have an inkling of it. Zombies come from villagers, and skeletons come from zombies. In ancient times, zombies and skeletons both knew this truth. Together they forged a weapon called the Bonesword to forever recognize this tie that bound them. The Bonesword was split into two parts, with one given to the skeletons and one to the zombies. But like so many ancient truths, its meaning was lost down the generations. The zombies kept their Bonesword in a special chamber and used it for ceremonies. But after a few thousand years, they thought that was all it was—a thing for ceremonies. In contrast, the ancient skeletons hid their Bonesword here, in the Fortress of Confusion, where it was protected by clever traps. Only someone with a great knowledge of skeleton lore—and some great crafting skills, to boot—would be able to find it. These measures were intended to keep the skeleton's Bonesword safe. Instead, because the traps and puzzles were so difficult to beat, it made them forget about it completely. As the years passed, the Fortress of Confusion became known as a strange place full of magical traps, but with no real purpose. It goes without saying, the true magic was forgotten."

"The true magic?" said Bacca.

"When the Boneswords were created, the zombies and skeletons poured into it all of the ancient magic they knew," said Tibia. "Individually, neither of the swords has any special power. But when they are *combined* with one another . . . it can unleash a mighty force that the Overworld has not seen in many ages."

"mmmm*How* do you know all of this?" asked Dug. The young zombie had no reason to doubt the skeleton, but the tale was so spectacular! It was a complete rewriting of everything he'd been taught in zombie history class.

"I know this because I have read the ancient books I found here," said Tibia, indicating the room with the library. "The books tell the story of how the Bonesword was forged. I have had many years to read them."

"mmmm*Why* are you even still here?" Dug pressed. "It doesn't seem like a very fun way to spend your time. The Skeleton King told us you ran away after he became king. That was thousands of years ago."

Tibia looked sad again.

"Do you know how the skeletons choose a leader?" the skeleton asked.

"Your brother mentioned some kind of contest," Bacca said.

"When the time comes for a new skeleton king or queen, candidates undergo the Trial of Fire," Tibia explained. "It involves several different challenges. An obstacle course. Various feats of strength. At one point, you even have to wrestle an iron golem! I won't bore you with the details. The important thing is that the final test—the one for which the trial takes its name—involves seeing who can stay out in the sunlight for an extended period of time. Given what sunlight does to skeletons, you can imagine how hard this is.

"The last time there was a Trial of Fire, only my brother and I were left at the final test. With the skeleton elders watching and our friends cheering us on, we walked out of the temple and into the bright sunshine. I thought that my brother's bones looked especially *shiny* that day. In the moment, I didn't think much of it. I was concentrating on the test. Maybe I thought he was just sweaty from wrestling the iron golem . . . which, looking back, should have made me very suspicious, because skeletons don't sweat. Anyway, I stayed out in the horrible, burning sunlight for as long as I could, but the pain became too severe. I felt myself drained to a fraction of a heart of life. I couldn't take it any longer, and I jumped back into the shade. My brother knew that he had won. He stayed there in the sun, and lifted his glistening arms above his head in victory.

"Only later that evening did it put it all together. His bones were glistening *because he had covered them with oil.* He cheated! The oil was protection from the sun. Now I knew he had not won at all, but by the time I realized this, it was too late. Skeleton coronations are practically instantaneous. When I saw my brother again, he had already washed all the evidence off his bones and they were putting the crown on his head."

Dug raised his brow in astonishment.

"mmmm*Then* that means you are . . . "

"The real Skeleton King," Bacca said.

Tibia nodded solemnly.

"mmmm What happened after your brother was crowned?" Dug asked.

"I ran away," said Tibia. "I didn't tell anybody where I was going. Many people thought I left for another biome, or for another server plane entirely. But I came here, to the Fortress of Confusion. I have lived here ever since. I tried to keep my hiding place a secret, but it seems that over the centuries the other skeletons have learned where I am."

"mmmm That's a sad story," Dug said.

"I try to make the best of it here," said Tibia. "There's plenty to read, and I've made friends with the magic sheep. He's part of the fortress, but he comes out to play every now and then."

"mmmm But it's not right. You should be king!"

"Yeah, I'm inclined to agree with Dug," Bacca said. "When I see that so-called Skeleton King again, he and I are going to have words. In the meantime, we really need to get the zombie's Bonesword back to them so that this needless fighting stops. So let's not waste any more ti—"

Bacca paused mid-sentence. Something had stopped him cold. The echo of strange footsteps unexpectedly reverberated behind them. Someone was walking up the ramp. Bacca, Dug, and Tibia looked at one another.

"Are you expecting anyone?" Bacca asked.

Tibia shook his head no.

Bacca put his finger to his lips to say they should all be quiet. Then he raised his diamond axe and crept near the edge of the ramp. For a moment, Bacca just listened. Whoever it was, they were walking slowly. Almost . . . zombishly slow. An idea occurred to Bacca, and he stuck his head around the corner to confirm it.

Loping up the ramp was a familiar-looking zombie in shining diamond armor.

"You!" Bacca said furiously, rising to his full height.

"mmmm*Wait,* I can explain!" Drooler said, lifting his upturned palms to beg for mercy.

"You've got a lot of nerve coming here!" Bacca continued.

Bacca stalked to where Drooler cowered and grabbed him by the scruff of the neck. Bacca marched him back up to Tibia and Dug.

"This is the one who caused all of this mess," Bacca said, plopping the zombie down in front of the skeleton. "He stole the Bonesword from the zombies because he thought they'd make him the new zombie king! Can you believe it?"

"mmmm*I* know," whimpered Drooler. "I'm so sorry. It was wrong!"

"What is he doing here?" Tibia asked.

Bacca had been so filled with rage at the sight of the zombie that he had not paused to ask this question. Now he thought it was a pretty good one.

"What *are* you doing here, Drooler?" Bacca pressed. "Explain yourself."

"mmmm*Something* new has happened. Something horrible. I need your help!"

"*You* want *our* help?" Bacca said. "After what you've done? Don't make me laugh."

"mmmm*Not* just me," Drooler said. "All the zombies are in trouble. Every zombie in Gravehome. And every person in the Overworld!"

"I'll give you 30 seconds to tell me more," Bacca said. "And this had better be good."

"mmmm*It's* the witches," Drooler stammered quickly. "They made a deal with The Spirit of the

Taiga. In return for a dragon egg—which, um, some-one gave it—the spirit agreed to clear the zombies out of Gravehome and give it to the witches. But I know those witches. They won't stop there. Once they figure out they can use The Spirit of the Taiga, they'll keep doing it. Nowhere will be safe. So I went and told the Skeleton King. He sent his troops to help defend Gravehome, but that might only hold them off for a while. The Spirit of the Taiga is very strong. I know there is also an old prophecy that one day the Bonesword will save the zombies in their hour of need. I think maybe this is that hour. So that's why I'm here."

There was a moment of silence as Drooler's words sank in. Bacca hated to admit it, but the situation did sound serious.

"My brother may be a cheater, but it was nice of him to send help," Tibia mused. "All things considered."

"I just hope it isn't too little, too late," Bacca said. "You don't mess with biome spirits. They are tough characters. As long as you stay on their good sides, they're fine. But once you make them angry . . . Let's just say it's a whole other ballgame."

"Our path is clear," Tibia said. "We must take the Boneswords—both of them—to Gravehome. With any luck, the swords' ancient magic will be enough to defeat The Spirit of the Taiga. Otherwise . . . Well, I don't want to think about the alternative."

Bacca quickly agreed. He didn't want to think about it either.

CHAPTER EIGHTEEN

G ravehome was under siege. The attacks against it were so ferocious that the very rocks comprising the mountain fortress seemed to shake and vibrate. Dust flew. Things fell over. Parts of the ceiling dislodged and crashed to the ground. More than once already, the Zombie King's crown had been jostled off of his head. (Because of this, he now carried it in his hand.)

"mmmm*Sire,* we must move you somewhere safer!" cried his guards.

But the king refused to move down to the dungeons. Neither would he consider making a break for it and escaping from Gravehome entirely. This was *his* fortress. This was the zombies' fortress, and he was their king. Whatever happened, he was going to stay right where he was.

For nearly a full day, the Spirit of the Taiga had been attacking Gravehome—throwing itself at the fortress as hard as it could. It started by running across the top of Gravehome, knocking over most of the cool-looking headstones that adorned the fortress. Then it jumped up and down on top of the mountain, causing it to vibrate in a terrifying manner. Then it felt for any soft spots in the fortress and dug madly into them, like a dog burying a bone—except the spirit was digging for zombies. Then it tried sticking its paws and muzzle into Gravehome's various entrances, trying to grab any zombies it could.

Several times, detachments of brave zombies had ventured out fight the spirit. And each time they had been beaten back. The Spirit of the Taiga stepped on the zombies with its enormous paws, and picked them up and flung them hundreds of feet away with its enormous jaws. (Being composed largely of rotting flesh, zombies were not particularly tasty. It was only for this reason that they avoided being eaten.) The zombies tried every weapon in their arsenal against the enormous wolf, but it seemed they could do no meaningful damage. After the tenth attack failed to result in anything other than smooshed zombies, the king had called them off.

The spirit's action had surprised and confused everyone, especially the king. Usually, biome spirits were peaceful, as long as you stayed out of their way. Sure, some had reputations as tricksters or liked to play pranks, but the Zombie King could not recall one being destructive for no reason. So what was this spirit up to?

The king got up from his throne, put his crown back on his head, and headed for one of Gravehome's upper exits.

"mmmmDon't go out there!" his attendants cried. "That thing is too powerful! It'll rip you to shreds!"

"mmmmIf I do nothing, it will rip this entire fortress to shreds!" the king retorted, and brushed past the other zombies. As the fortress shook and shuddered under the spirit's violent attacks, the king wound his way up through the tunnels that took him near the surface. He opened a hatch in the ceiling, and crawled out into a once-ornate mausoleum on the side of Gravehome. The Spirit of the Taiga had recently smashed it to ruins.

The Zombie King got his bearings and saw the Spirit of the Taiga throwing its shoulder into the side of the fortress. It took several steps back, then ran forward at full tilt until it crashed into the fortress wall. Then it did it again.

"mmmm*Hey*!" cried the king. "Come over here and talk to me . . . you, you . . . overgrown hound!"

The Spirit of the Taiga looked to see who had addressed it. Then its eyes lit on the king and it smiled evilly. The spirit loped up the side of the mountain until it stood beside the Zombie King. The giant wolf towered over the zombie. The spirit was panting hard from all its violent activity. Its hot breath fogged the air around the king.

"mmmm*Why* are you doing this to us?" demanded the king. "We zombies have no quarrel with you. Did *the skeletons* put you up to this?"

The spirit laughed. The king was surrounded by even more fog.

"The skeletons?" it said. "What are you talking about? I don't know anything about any skeletons. I'm not doing this for them."

"mmmm*Then* why?" said the king.

"Let's just say that someone gave me a present I liked," said the spirit. "I agreed to do a favor in return for that present. And that favor just happened to be clearing all of the zombies out of Gravehome."

The king was baffled. Clearing all the zombies out of Gravehome? It was unthinkable! How could he stop this from happening?

"mmmm*What* if *I* gave you a gift?" the king said, thinking quickly. "There's got to be something in our treasury that you want!"

"My current employer gave me a Dragon Egg," bragged the spirit. "Have you got anything that beats a Dragon Egg?"

"mmmm*I* . . . Um . . . Uh . . . " the Zombie King hesitated. He did a quick mental inventory of all the baubles in his treasury. The king had many exotic items, but nothing quite like that.

Suddenly, a loud voice sounded from the foot of the mountain below them.

"Don't you give that jerk anything!"

Both the king and the spirit turned, and both were astonished by what they saw.

While they had been talking, an enormous skeleton army had moved into place in front of Gravehome. There were thousands of skeleton troops of all types. Skeletons wearing heavy armor readied themselves for a frontal assault. Skeleton spider jockeys had massed into cavalry formation, and were preparing to charge. And of course there were archers—thousands and thousands of skeleton archers stood in formations stretching back nearly to the horizon!

Leading this enormous army was the Skeleton King. He was wearing battle armor and an armored crown.

"Hey doggie doggie doggie," the Skeleton King clicked tauntingly. "Someone told us you were looking for a fight. Why don't you leave those zombies alone and come play with us for a while?"

The Spirit of the Taiga did not like being referred to as "doggie." He glared at the Skeleton King and his eyes narrowed. The Skeleton King stretched out the string of his bow like an athlete warming up before a big game. The Spirit of the Taiga had never seen these skeletons before. He didn't know why they'd come to pick a fight with him. They were certainly not involved in his agreement to clear out Gravehome.

But they had said it. The dreaded "D-word." There could be no turning back.

Certainly—the Spirit of the Taiga thought to itself—there must be time to take a little break from attacking Gravehome to deal with these rude visitors.

"Hey doggie," the Skeleton King said. "Did you hear me? I'm talking to *you!*"

The king nocked and arrow and let it fly. It struck the spirit right on the tip of the nose, one of the only places its thick fur did not offer protection.

The Spirit of the Taiga angrily brushed aside the Zombie King with its enormous paw. The king was not expecting this, and flew headlong into a tombstone.

Then the spirit leaped down the side of the fortress into the fields of skeletons below. Thousands of arrows sailed through the air. One set of giant teeth gnashed. Little bits of broken skeleton began to fly.

The Zombie King hardly had time to think. Clutching his head, which he'd banged on the tombstone, he crawled back through the hatch into Gravehome.

"mmmm*Generals!* Generals!" he called at the top of his voice.

They were right there. All of his top generals— and everybody else on his staff—had gathered below the hatch to see what was happening.

"mmmm*Generals* . . . get every zombie you can spare!" the king cried. "Open the gates and charge!"

"mmmm*Sire?*" one said, as though afraid he had not heard the king correctly.

"mmmm*There's* no time to explain!" the king cried. "This is the best chance we'll ever have to defeat the spirit. And if you see any skeletons—"

"mmmm*We* should fight them, too?" asked a zombie general.

"mmmm*No!*" said the king. "You should help them in any way you can!"

The generals were too astounded to speak. Wondering if their leader had gone completely insane, they rushed off through the hallways of Gravehome to muster their troops.

Meanwhile . . .

Bacca, Dug, Drooler, and Tibia hurried across the Overworld in the direction of Gravehome.

Bacca found that he was naturally much faster than the three undead compatriots who now comprised his party. Luckily for Bacca, his inventory was full of Potions of Swiftness. Whenever the zombies and skeletons drank the potions, they were almost able to keep up with Bacca. Almost being the key word.

"C'mon you guys," Bacca urged. "We're very close. Have another potion. Gravehome is in the next biome."

"Sorry," said Tibia. "I'd been in that fortress for thousands of years. I'm a little out of practice when it comes to *running across the Overworld at full speed.*"

Bacca thought he detected a bit of sarcasm. The old jumble of bones still had some spark left in him after all these years. It made Bacca smile.

"mmmm*I* don't understand what we're going to do when we *get* to Gravehome," Dug said.

"The Spirit of the Taiga is a really tough character," said Bacca. "We're going to need everything in our power to defeat him. Maybe armies of skeletons and zombies working together will be enough. And maybe Betty and I can do it. But probably, we're going to be really glad that we have the Bonesword with us. I don't know if I believe in prophecies, but it sure looks like now's the right time for the Bonesword to do its thing."

"That sounds good to me," said Tibia. "And after we're done with that, I've got a bone to pick with my brother. Literally."

"By the way," Bacca said. "When we *do* combine the two Boneswords—the skeleton one and the zombie one—into a single sword . . . ?"

"Yes?" said the skeleton.

"What happens?" Bacca asked.

He had no lips, but Bacca could have sworn that the skeleton was smiling.

"Something very mystical and powerful," said Tibia. "Something magical. Something that is a little different each time, and depends on the situation."

Bacca opened his mouth to say that this answer could have been clearer, but then thought better of it. Gravehome was already looming into view ahead of them. At the same moment, the ground beneath their feet began showing signs of having been recently trampled by a skeleton army that must number in the thousands. From up ahead, they began to hear the sound of zombie and skeleton voices raised in the pitch of battle.

"We're almost there!" Bacca shouted.

A little further, and they began to encounter the edges of the battle. The skeletons had set up a triage tent where zombie medics reassembled skeletons that had been bashed apart or had bones broken by the Spirit of the Taiga.

Past this tent was the battle itself.

An army of zombies and skeletons had completely encircled Gravehome. They were no longer pursuing any kind of tactical maneuver—as far as Bacca could tell, at least—because the Spirit of the Taiga was so fast and so enormous that it made any kind of coordinated assault impossible. The zombies and skeletons could not act, only react. The angry spirit leapt all around the fortress, throwing itself angrily at the troops. It attacked with all four paws, and caught soldiers in its jaws and flung them with a flick of its head. The soldiers only had a chance to swing their weapons if the enormous wolf chanced to get close enough. The skeleton archers fired many arrows, but the spirit was fast-moving and hard to hit. The vast majority of them missed.

Despite these challenges, Bacca was cheered to see that the zombies and skeletons had made some progress. The tip of the spirit's nose was full of so many skeleton arrows that it looked like a pincushion. Its fiery red eyes burned with an intense hatred, and it looked very angry. *Very* angry. One look told Bacca that this was no longer a favor for some witches. Now it was personal.

"Quick," Bacca said. "Let's use the sword. Now or never."

"It is not that easy," said Tibia.

"What?" said Bacca. "*Not that easy?* Why not?"

"According to the prophecy, not just anybody can wield the combined Bonesword," said Tibia. "It has to be the leader of the skeletons and the leader of the zombies . . . *at the same time.*"

"mmmm*How* can you swing a sword at the same time?" Drooler interrupted. "What if one person wanted to swing it one direction, and the other person wanted to swing it the other way?"

"Quiet, you," Bacca said. "You're only here because I can't figure out what to do with you yet."

"mmmm*Sorry,*" said Drooler timidly.

"Have no fear," Tibia said cryptically. "When the Bonesword is activated, you won't need to worry about swinging it."

"Okaaaaaay," said Bacca. "So let's go find the people we need to make that happen."

Their group began to sprint across the chaotic battlefield. They were close enough that they were in danger of becoming a part of the action. The zombie and skeleton troops around them were readying themselves for the spirit's next pass.

Suddenly, Dug said, "mmmm*There!* Look! The Skeleton King!"

Dug gestured frantically to a spot on the battlefield where a particularly regal-looking skeleton in special armor was readying an arrow in an enormous bow. Bacca hurried over to him just as he let the arrow fly.

"Drat!" said the Skeleton King. "Another miss. That cursed thing moves so fast!"

"Your highness!" Bacca said.

"Ahh, Bacca!" exclaimed the king. "I see you survived the Fortress of Confusion, and so did your zombie friend, and . . . and . . . who are these . . . ?"

The king's voice faltered as his eyes fell upon his brother.

"Yes," said Bacca. "We're all here, safe and sound. The important thing is that we found the Bonesword."

Bacca quickly explained what they had learned about the Bonesword's special power, and how it was really two swords in one.

"Why, this is all quite surprising," said the Skeleton King.

"No kidding," Bacca said. "But let's talk about all that later. Now, we need to focus on defeating that enormous wolf over there. For the Bonesword to work, you and the Zombie King have to hold the two halves of it at the same time when they're joined. Do you know where the Zombie King is?"

"I saw him go back inside Gravehome as our army arrived," said the king. "I haven't seen him since. For all I know, he's still there."

"Fine," Bacca said, turning to Dug and the others. "The three of you stay here with the Skeleton King and get the Bonesword ready. I'm going into Gravehome to find the Zombie King."

With that, the furry crafter dashed off through the thick of the battlefield toward the nearest entrance to the fortress. He dodged through the lines of soldiers, sometimes leaping over them in a single bound, until he came to the fortress door, where a sentry barred his way.

"I don't have time to explain, but I need to see the king!" Bacca shouted. When the guard opened his mouth to object, Bacca faked left and went right, a classic move that worked perfectly. The guard's head spun as Bacca raced past him into Gravehome.

Retracing the path from his previous visit, Bacca made his way to the Zombie King's throne room. As Bacca hurried inside, he saw immediately why the king was not on the battlefield. The throne room was full of worried-looking zombies, and the king was lying on the floor in front of his throne. He had sustained some kind of serious injury to his head. Bacca was not an expert on zombie injuries—beyond knowing that if he gave zombies enough whacks with a diamond axe they were done for—but Bacca decided that the Zombie King on the floor didn't look so great.

Bacca hurried over. The king motioned that his attendants should make way for Bacca. Soon, the hairy crafter stood right beside the wounded zombie.

"mmmm *You* have returned!" the king exclaimed. Though he was delighted to see Bacca, the king's voice was very weak.

"Yes, and I have good news," Bacca said. "We recovered the Bonesword. Actually, it turns out it's Bone*swords,* plural. Funny story, that . . ."

Bacca gave the king a rundown of his travels with Dug, and how they had been able to retrieve the Bonesword. Even though time was of the essence, Bacca spared no detail. The king visibly relaxed as Bacca spoke, and some of the anguish left his ancient face.

"mmmm *You* have no idea how much this pleases me," the king said when Bacca was finished with his tale. "The guards you sent back from Rotpit confessed their part in the crime, but we did not know if we should believe them. Now they—and especially Drooler—can be brought to justice."

The king let out a very deep moan. At first, Bacca assumed the ruler was giving orders to the zombies around him. Yet their faces showed no comprehension. Bacca realized it was a moan of pain.

"mmmm*But* that justice," the king continued, "may happen under a different monarch. The Spirit of the Taiga threw me against a headstone. I am badly wounded."

"I think we can defeat the spirit using the Bonesword," Bacca said. "The prophecy surrounding the sword is real, but we need your help. Are you well enough to come out onto the battlefield? I could carry you if you like."

"mmmm*You* misunderstand the gravity of my situation," the king said. "My remaining time might be measured in seconds. But listen! This is important. What you have told me of the accomplishments of your student Dug has changed my mind. At first, I was unsure what to think of a zombie crafter. After hearing your tale, I think that there may be no one better suited to lead the zombies in their hour of need!"

Several of the zombies in the room moaned in shock at the king's words.

The king chuckled to himself, amused at how scandalized they were.

"mmmm*It* is permitted in our tradition for a zombie king or queen to choose their successor," the king continued. "With my final breath, I decree that your student, Dug the zombie, is the new . . . Zombie . . . King."

The old king's eyes closed. His jaw dropped open, and the undead life went out of his body. Some of the zombies in the throne room took off their helmets out of respect.

As was traditional, some of them chanted: "mmmm*The* king is undead, long live the king! The king is undead, long live the king!"

Then one of them seemed to realize something and said: "mmmm*By* the way, where *is* our new king?"

Bacca—who was already halfway out the door—shouted, "Follow me and you'll find out!"

CHAPTER NINETEEN

Back outside of Gravehome, the battle raged on. The Spirit of the Taiga was getting angrier and angrier by the moment. There were even more zombie arrows sticking out of its snout.

Bacca bounded over the rows battling soldiers until he arrived once again back at the side of the Skeleton King.

"What happened?" cried Tibia, alarmed at seeing Bacca return alone. "Is everything all right? Where is the Zombie King?"

"You're looking at him," Bacca replied with a smile.

"What?" Tibia said.

The skeleton looked around, but failed to see anything.

"Look a little lower," Bacca said.

The skeleton still didn't get it. Apparently, none of them did.

"mmmm*Is* he invisible?" Dug tried.

Bacca shook his head and laughed.

"No Dug," Bacca said. "He's you. You're the new Zombie King."

"mmmm*Huh*?" Dug said. "I think I misheard you, Bacca. It sounded like you said that I was the new zombie king."

"That's because I did," Bacca replied. "*You are the new zombie king.* As the old king died, he named you as his successor. I just saw it happen. So did all the zombies in the king's court."

"mmmm*But* . . . but . . . " Dug said, quite bewildered by this turn of events.

"There'll be time for it to sink in later," Bacca reassured him. "Right now, all you need to do is grab hold of your half of the Bonesword."

Bacca turned to Tibia.

"All right, Tibia. Let's make this happen. What do they do with the swords?"

"It's very simple," the skeleton said. "Dug holds the zombie Bonesword, my brother holds the other one. Then they fit them together and point it at the Spirit of the Taiga."

"That's it?" Bacca said.

"That's it," confirmed Tibia.

"Then what are we waiting for?" said Bacca enthusiastically.

They took out the two Boneswords and gave the one with zombies etched on the blade to Dug, and the one with skeleton carvings to the Skeleton King. They were shaped to fit together perfectly, like two pieces of the same puzzle, to form a larger, even more impressive-looking sword.

"mmmm*Wait*," Dug said, raising a rotting hand. "The Spirit of the Taiga is way over there, on the other side of the battlefield. I don't know what exactly is going to happen when we do this . . . but what if we *miss* because he's so far off?"

"I'll get him closer," Bacca said confidently.

Bacca put two claws in his mouth and blew. A whistling sound echoed so loudly that the soldiers covered their ears (or ear holes, in the case of skeletons). They stopped fighting and looked at Bacca. The Spirit of the Taiga looked too.

"Get over here!" Bacca cried at the top of his lungs. "You . . . *mutt!*"

The Spirit of the Taiga's eyes blazed red and locked on Bacca. Bacca smiled and waved. Then he blew the enormous beast a kiss. The spirit went mad with rage and began to charge. It thundered across the battlefield. The ground shook at its approach.

"Okay," Bacca called. "I think now would be a good time to combine the swords. Guys? Guys, can you hear me? I said, I think that now would be—"

"mmmm*We* are!" Dug cried from behind him.

Bacca turned and looked. Much to his alarm, Bacca saw that Dug was telling the truth. They had fit the swords together. Doing so had indeed created a much larger, majestic-looking weapon. But there was no magical effect that Bacca could see. Both Dug and the Skeleton King were holding fast to the weapon's hilt, and nothing was happening.

Meanwhile, the Spirit of the Taiga drew closer.

Despite the situation, Bacca had to grin.

"I thought this might be the case," he said. "Tibia? Why don't *you* try holding the sword instead?"

"But . . . but . . . " stammered the Skeleton King.

"mmmm*Just* do what he says," Dug interjected. "The Spirit of the Taiga is almost here!"

And it was.

The enormous beast galloped ever-closer. It knocked over hundreds of skeleton and zombie soldiers on its way, yet paid them no mind. They were only incidental now. Its real target—its *only* target—was whatever that hairy thing was in the suit that had called it a *mutt.*

Fueled by rage, the spirit's vision narrowed into a pinhole, until the only thing it saw was Bacca. The spirit could hear nothing beside its own angry breath in its ears. Soon it was very close to Bacca. Then closer still.

With the moon high in the sky behind it, the Spirit of the Taiga cast a long shadow. In the moment that the shadow reached the group holding the Bonesword—with the spirit itself barreling *very* close behind—there was a shuffling in the people standing by the hairy crafter. A rearrangement of some kind. The skeleton who had been holding the sword let go . . . and a different skeleton grabbed the weapon.

And the result was instantaneous.

CHAPTER TWENTY

acca, Dug, Tibia, Drooler, and the erstwhile king of the skeletons could hardly believe what they were seeing.

In one moment, the enormous scary wolf had been careening down on top of them, so near they could smell its breath. In the next moment, the enormous beast seemed to have completely disappeared!

Dug and Tibia were so stunned that each dropped his half of the Bonesword. It separated and fell to the earth with two soft clunks. Steam was rising off both halves.

"mmmm *Wow*!" said Dug. "That rotten wolf just disappeared! How cool!"

"It *was* pretty cool," Bacca said, bending down to investigate the steaming swords. They were hot to the touch.

"mmmm *I* guess the prophecy was real after all," Dug said. "When the king of the zombies and the king of the skeletons work together, they can use the Bonesword to unleash truly incredible magic!"

"Then that means . . . that means . . . " said the skeleton wearing the armored crown of finger bones. "That means that this is really yours. You are the true Skeleton King."

He took off the crown and handed it to his brother. Tibia accepted the crown, and carefully placed it on his own head. Even though he was a skeleton, and making subtle expressions wasn't a particular skeleton strength, it was easy to see how proud Tibia was.

The old king looked downcast.

"I'm so sorry I cheated in the Trial of Fire all those years ago," he said. "You were always better at standing in the sunlight than me. I knew you were going to win, and that's why I cheated. I shouldn't have done it. All this time, I've felt rotten about it."

"I *thought* the Bonesword would be able to tell," Bacca interjected. "It looks like I was right."

"I forgive you for cheating," Tibia said to his brother. "You're not a bad person, you just got tempted and made a mistake. Promise that you won't do it again."

"I won't!" said the former king. "I've learned my lesson. From now on, I'll be honest in everything I do."

The skeleton troops nearby heard this exchange. They began cheering and chanting: "Long live the king! Long live the king!" Tibia put his hand in the air and waved to them. All of the skeletons broke into bony applause. Bacca was happy for Tibia, and also decided things probably wouldn't be so bad for the old Skeleton King. After all, skeletons were much more interested in celebrating a new king than criticizing a former one.

Next, a large contingent of zombies headed their way. It was the generals and other high-ranking zombies from the king's court. They had come out onto the battlefield. The one in front was holding a crown the color of rotting flesh.

As Bacca looked on, the zombies put the crown firmly on Dug's head, and stepped a few paces away.

Dug was stunned.

"mmmm*Pssst*," he whispered to Bacca. "What do I do?"

"Tell them thank you," Bacca said. "Then tell them whatever you want. You're their king now. They do what *you* say."

"mmmm*Thank* you," Dug said to the zombie that had crowned him. Then all the zombies broke into moan-y cheers. Dug tried to wave to them—like Tibia had—but he was too short to be seen above the gathering crowd. Bacca picked Dug up and put him on his shoulders. Now the crowd could see Dug easily, and they all cheered again.

Eventually, after lots of cheering, Bacca set Dug back down.

"mmmm*I* can't believe we did it!" said the new zombie king. "Not only did we stop the war, but we also saved Gravehome, got the Bonesword, and—most importantly—learned about the shared history between all zombies and skeletons."

"Yes," said Bacca. "A good week's work, I think. It looks like everything is all wrapped up."

Then something across the battlefield caught Bacca's eye.

"Except for maybe one thing . . ." he added mysteriously.

Dug turned and looked.

Crawling across the floor of the battlefield was a very small dog—the kind that might sit on a tiny cushion beside a king, or that a queen might carry in her purse. It was crawling between pieces of discarded armor—hiding under a dented helmet, shielding itself between broken breastplates. It gave the distinct impression of trying very hard not to be seen.

"Ha!" Bacca exclaimed. "It looks like the Bonesword didn't make the Spirit of the Taiga disappear completely. It just shrunk him down to size. And then some!"

Pushing aside the zombies and skeletons who surrounded their new leaders, Bacca jogged across the battlefield until he reached the tiny canine. It was shivering underneath an iron helmet. Even though it was trying to hide, its tail stuck out from underneath. It wasn't fooling anybody.

Bacca leaned over and picked it up. The small beast struggled as Bacca held it up to look it in the eyes.

"Got you!" Bacca said.

"Ack!" said the former spirit. "This is my worst fear. I've become a regular dog!"

"You realize it serves you right, don't you?" Bacca said. "You were doing horrible things to people, just because those witches gave you a Dragon Egg. Look around here. Look at all the chaos you caused!"

"I know," said the tiny dog. "I'm sorry. Please don't eat me or anything."

Bacca laughed.

"Since the Bonesword didn't turn you into a delicious raw fish, you won't have to worry about that," he said.

"Then what are you going to do to me?" the small dog said, shaking with fear.

"mmmm*I* have some ideas for that," a voice said.

It was Dug. He had caught up with Bacca. Marching next to him was a group of zombie soldiers. In the center of this group was Drooler. Someone had put leg-irons on his legs.

"mmmm*You* two *deserve each other*," Dug said to both Drooler and the Spirit of the Taiga. "As punishment for your evil actions, I require that you live here at Gravehome as prisoners—until such time as I feel you have learned your lessons. Drooler, you will be responsible for taking this doggie for regular walks, picking the fleas out of his fur, and giving him regular baths."

"Treated like a dog!" moaned the former Spirit of the Taiga. "The ultimate humiliation!"

"mmmm*Pet* care moves me much further down the line from being the next king of the zombies," moaned Drooler.

"I'd say it moves you just about to last place," Bacca said. "But you should have thought of that before you started a war and tried to steal the zombie throne."

Bacca took a slimeball and four pieces of string out of his inventory. He used them to craft a lead. Then he put the lead around the tiny dog's neck, and handed the other end to Drooler.

"Here you go," Bacca said. "You two better make the best of it. You're going to be friends for a very long time."

Drooler reluctantly took the lead from Bacca, and slowly walked his new pet away.

Tibia approached. He was holding both halves of the Bonesword. It had finally stopped steaming.

"What are we going to do with this?" Tibia asked.

"Why don't you and Dug work that out?" Bacca suggested. "After all, you're the new kings."

"mmmm*I* have an idea," said Dug. "We can each hold onto our half of it, like in ancient times. We can send for the other if we need to use it. That way, it will only be used for important stuff. Both zombies and skeletons will have to be in agreement. The way it should be."

"Like it was before," Tibia said. "Like the creators intended."

"Yes," said Dug. "But this time, we won't forget what the Bonesword does. It's not just a pretty thing for ceremonies. It has real power. And we will be careful to treat it like that, and to always keep it safe. For example, no more keeping it on a platform with just a couple of guards. It needs to be more secure than that. Personally, I'm going to craft a special locked, trapped chest to keep our half of it in. It will be my finest crafting achievement."

"I like that idea," said Tibia. "I see that there will be some advantages for the zombies in having a king who is also a master crafter."

Bacca often told prospective students that crafting was important for all sorts of career fields one could go into. Now, apparently, he could add government and politics to that list. Who would have thought?

Dug turned to Bacca.

"mmmm*As* king, my first responsibility needs to be repairing Gravehome from the damage caused by this battle," said Dug. "But I won't just give orders. Using my crafting skills, I'll personally help rebuild it stronger and better than before."

"I'm sure you will," Bacca said to Dug. "I'm very proud of what you're doing. Throughout all of this, you've proven that zombies can be as skilled as anyone else when it comes to crafting. I think the parents of my crafting students—the ones who criticized the idea of zombie crafters—are going to find themselves with little to complain about when they hear about your accomplishments."

"mmmm*Speaking* of your class," Dug said. "I'll have to miss the rest to do these repairs. But I think we can be finished in time for me to come back for graduation."

"That sounds fine," Bacca said. "We will look forward to that."

"Thanks again, Bacca. I'll be seeing you," Dug said, sending his mentor off with a wave.

Bacca had no doubt that Dug would make good on his word.

CHAPTER TWENTY-ONE

Several weeks later, at the end of the summer, Bacca and LadyBacc prepared to bestow the Bacca-laureate degree on all the students who had successfully completed their crafting class. On the front grounds of Bacca's castle, LadyBacc had crafted a beautiful stage across which the graduates would march. They would shake hands with Bacca and LadyBacc, and then receive a diploma and a set of special crafting tools.

Students' families had come from all across the Overworld to pick up their young crafters and watch the graduation. Many of the family members used this as an excuse to meet Bacca personally. He was, after all, one of the Overworld's most famous celebrities. Between shaking hands and wishing the crafters well, Bacca took special care to spend time with Dug's parents. Bacca and LadyBacc had built a special shade canopy so the zombies would not be burned by the sun while they watched the ceremony, which everyone found very considerate. It turned out that Dug's parents did not live in Gravehome, so they'd heard about Dug's becoming king secondhand.

"mmmm*At* first, we didn't believe it!" Dug's father told Bacca. "We thought someone was playing a joke on us. Can you imagine? Hearing that your boy— who you just dropped off at crafting camp—had become king a week later? My head spun! Literally. It can do that because I'm a zombie. Want to see?"

Dug's father showed Bacca how he could rotate his head a full 360 degrees. Bacca nodded and tried not to throw up. Zombies could be a little weird, sometimes.

When it was time for the ceremony, Bacca and LadyBacc read each young crafter's name and what their final project had been while the crafter walked across the stage to receive his or her diploma. After each diploma was given out, the audience applauded politely. Soon, all of the students had received their diplomas except for one—a short, bluish-green one who was wearing a crown. It was a little too big for him, and hung crookedly off the side of his head. Bacca secretly thought this was adorable. Bacca cleared his throat and prepared to read the final entry.

"And, for a final project that included investigating the theft of the Bonesword, scaling the hut of the three witches, solving the mysteries of the Fortress of Confusion, and defeating the Spirit of the Taiga . . . we hereby award this Bacca-laureate degree to Dug, the Zombie King."

All of the families seated in front of the stage stood up and broke into loud applause and cheers. Bacca had never seen a zombie blush—he did not know if it was physically possible—but he could have sworn that Dug's cheeks turned slightly red as he walked across the stage to receive his diploma and tools.

"Well done!" Bacca said to the young zombie. "I'm very proud of you!"

"mmmm*Thanks*," said Dug with a smile. "I couldn't have done it without your help!"

"I'm also very proud of you!" said LadyBacc, shaking Dug's hand next.

"mmmm*Thank* you," said Dug. "I learned a great deal from you as well!"

Bacca was so happy for Dug that he also cheered. He knew that this wasn't the end for his student, but just the beginning of a whole new series of crafting adventures. He was excited to see what the young Zombie King would do next. It was going to be great fun finding out!

After the graduation ceremony was over, the crafters and their families said goodbye to Bacca and LadyBacc and gradually departed. (This included Dug, who had convinced his parents to move to the zombie capital with him.) Bacca and LadyBacc stood next to each other and waved as everyone began their long journeys home. As the last of the crafters faded into the distance, Bacca and LadyBacc prepared to break down the stage and clean up the lawn where the ceremony had been held. It wasn't glamorous work, but still important to do.

"Wow," LadyBacc said. "What a summer! I doubt we'll ever have a crafting class that interesting again."

"I dunno," Bacca said. "Never say never. Living on the Overworld has taught me not to be too sure about anything."

No sooner were these words out of Bacca's mouth than a strange glow began to appear in the shadows next to where he stood. Both Bacca and LadyBacc stopped and watched it, mesmerized. Several bits of glowing purple matter had materialized out of nowhere. They were about the size of leaves, and, like leaves, were blown about by the wind.

Gradually, the glowing purple bits seemed to coalesce, forming a jet black creature with a square head and bright purple eyes. The creature had long legs and even longer arms that reached down almost to its feet. Purple glowing bits continued to swirl around its body, even as it stood there.

"An Enderman!" said LadyBacc, preparing to draw a weapon. "What's it doing here? I know they can teleport, but I've never seen one teleport this far aboveground."

"Let's see what it wants before we get defensive," Bacca cautioned.

The Enderman looked around—surveying Bacca's castle, the lawns, and the graduation stage—until its glowing purple eyes finally lit on Bacca and LadyBacc. It awkwardly lumbered toward them.

"Are you the one called Bacca?" it asked in a strange, otherworldly voice.

"I am," Bacca said. "And this is my girlfiend, LadyBacc."

"Pleased to meet you," the enderman said. "My name is Pearl."

Bacca reached up and shook the hand at the end of its creepily-long arm. "Pearl" was an interesting name for an enderman. Bacca wondered if there were Enderwomen too. Apparently so.

"I know Endermen don't usually come to this part of the Overworld, but I have special request," the creature continued. "I have a daughter who is very interested in becoming a crafter. She takes it very seriously. Being able to study with a true master of crafting would mean so much to her. So I was wondering if perhaps . . . um . . . "

"We would be *happy* to give you an application for next summer's crafting class," Bacca said.

"Oh, thank you!" said the Enderman, clearly overjoyed. "My daughter will be so pleased. Crafting is all she talks about."

"There's a stack of applications just inside my castle," Bacca said. "Hang on. We'll be right back."

Bacca and LadyBacc walked to the office where Bacca kept the application forms. The Enderman waited outside and beamed with pleasure. The bright purple light coming from its eyes seemed to radiate happiness.

"See? It looks like our class could be even more interesting next year," Bacca said.

"I guess you're right," LadyBacc said. "And that sounds just fine to me."

Then something seemed to occur to her.

"You know," she said. "Now that I think about it, it seemed like you and Dug tied up all the loose ends in your adventure with the zombies and skeletons . . . except for one."

"Hmm?" Bacca said, looking through his desk for the application forms.

"Those horrible witches," LadyBacc said. "They were the ones who brought the Spirit of the Taiga into it. They acted like real monsters, if you ask me—trying to kick the zombies out of Gravehome so they could have it. That part was all their fault."

"I agree," said Bacca. "It was. That's why I paid them a visit on my way back home from the battle."

"You *did*?" asked LadyBacc.

Bacca nodded.

"Yes," he said. "Let's just say that those witches won't be bothering anybody else for a very long time."

LadyBacc smiled, happy to know the matter had been resolved.

Together, they found the applications and brought one back outside to the excited Enderman. (Or Enderwoman.) Bacca didn't know what next year's class-members would look like, but he knew one thing for sure: He couldn't wait to meet them!

EPILOGUE

Flappy the bat could not believe his good fortune.

First, he'd returned home from an ingredient-retrieving errand to find that all the witches had disappeared from the hut. Instead of being criticized for finding the wrong ingredient—or for not bringing back enough of it—the witches had not been there at all. Which, Flappy found to his surprise, he actually liked very much. For the rest of the evening and most of the following day, Flappy had lounged about the chicken leg hut, with no responsibilities at all. Doing this was incredibly relaxing. He wondered why he hadn't tried it sooner.

Then, by chance, he'd noticed the note.

Opening the front door of the hut to see if the witches might be coming back from that direction, Flappy saw that a small piece of paper had been nailed to the hut's front door. Unlike most bats, Flappy could read and write. Years spent around the witches had made this necessary, as he always had to jot down the complicated lists of ingredients they wanted him to find.

Curious, Flappy took down the note and began to read it. It said:

The finder of this note is entitled to become the new owner of this hut, and everything inside. The witches who used to live here have volunteered to take a permanent vacation to the Fortress of Confusion, where they have agreed to live out the remainder of their days without hurting anybody else, ever again.

Thank you for taking care of this hut, and not using any of the potions inside to hurt people.

Signed,
Bacca

Flappy launched himself off the front of the hut and did happy circles in the air. His own hut! All for him! Where he could do whatever he wanted, whenever he wanted, with no witches to answer to!

Now he would spend all his time lounging around or looking for yummy insects to eat, instead of going on endless boring errands for the witches. Flappy couldn't imagine anything nicer.

Whoever this mysterious "Bacca" person was, Flappy decided he must be all right.

About the Author

JeromeASF is an Internet personality created by Jerome Aceti, best known for his YouTube Minecraft videos and his character Bacca. Since it was created in 2011, the JeromeASF channel (www.youtube.com/JeromeASF) has grown to become one of the leading YouTube Minecraft channels around the world, with millions of subscribers and hundreds of millions of views.

DO YOU LIKE FICTION FOR MINECRAFTERS?

Check out other unofficial Minecrafter adventures from Mark Cheverton and Sky Pony Press!

The Gameknight999 Series

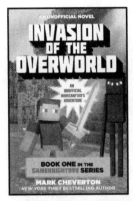

Invasion of the Overworld

Battle for the Nether

Confronting the Dragon

Available wherever books are sold!

DO YOU LIKE FICTION FOR MINECRAFTERS?

Check out other unofficial Minecrafter adventures from Mark Cheverton and Sky Pony Press!

The Mystery of Herobrine Series

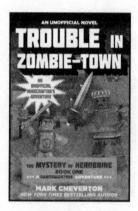

Trouble in
Zombie-town

The Jungle
Temple Oracle

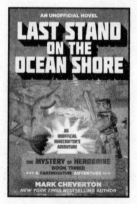

Last Stand on
the Ocean Shore

Available wherever books are sold!

DO YOU LIKE FICTION FOR MINECRAFTERS?

Check out other unofficial Minecrafter adventures from Winter Morgan and Sky Pony Press!

The Unofficial Gamer's Adventure Series

The Quest for the Diamond Sword

The Mystery of the Griefer's Mark

The Endermen Invasion

Available wherever books are sold!

DO YOU LIKE FICTION FOR MINECRAFTERS?

Check out other unofficial Minecrafter adventures from Winter Morgan and Sky Pony Press!

The Unofficial Gamer's Adventure Series

Treasure Hunters
in Trouble

The Skeletons
Strike Back

Clash of the
Creepers

DO YOU LIKE FICTION FOR MINECRAFTERS?

Check out other unofficial Minecrafter adventures from Winter Morgan and Sky Pony Press!

The Unofficial League of Griefers Adventure Series

The Secret
Treasure

Hidden in the
Overworld

The Griefer's
Revenge

DO YOU LIKE FICTION FOR MINECRAFTERS?

Check out other unofficial Minecrafter adventures from Winter Morgan and Sky Pony Press!

The Unofficial League of Griefers Adventure Series

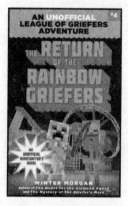

The Return of the Rainbow Griefers

The Nether Attack

The Hardcore War